"I've been wanting all morning to kiss you."

"And I don't want to wait any longer," Sara said to Drew.

She lowered her lips to his and his arms encircled her, pulling her down onto him. She angled her mouth more firmly against his and threaded her fingers through his hair. His lips caressed sensitive nerve endings, sending waves of pleasure through her.

She opened her mouth, inviting his tongue, reveling in the feel of him, tasting of sweetness and salt. He smelled of seawater, and his skin beneath her hands was rough with sand.

He smoothed his hands down her back, caressing her skin, lingering over the indentation at the bottom of her spine, shaping his f...... to her buttocks and squeezing g....... ache of desire welled in ..... her breath at its i........ remember when .... way.

She broke the kiss a........ at him.

He reached up to bru..... her hair back from her forehead and said, "I want to see you naked... now."

Blaze™

Dear Reader,

We've all heard about male bonding, but I believe female bonding is what truly holds the world together. There's nothing like female friendship. Which is why writing *Wild Child* was extra special for me. Not only did I get to write a book in a miniseries about three close female friends, but I also got to do it with two friends of mine, Dawn Atkins and Colleen Collins.

Dawn, Colleen and I brainstormed this story a couple of years ago, and gradually it evolved into the SEX ON THE BEACH miniseries, of which *Wild Child* is the third book. If you haven't read the other two books—*Swept Away* by Dawn Atkins and *Shock Waves* by Colleen Collins—do find them. You're in for a treat.

Friendship, fun, sun and hot guys—what else do you need for a great vacation? I hope this story is a fun vacation from your everyday life. I'd love to hear from you. You can find me online at www.CindiMyers.com.

Happy reading!

Cindi Myers

WILD CHILD
Cindi Myers

TORONTO • NEW YORK • LONDON
AMSTERDAM • PARIS • SYDNEY • HAMBURG
STOCKHOLM • ATHENS • TOKYO • MILAN • MADRID
PRAGUE • WARSAW • BUDAPEST • AUCKLAND

ISBN-13: 978-0-373-79364-8
ISBN-10:   0-373-79364-2

WILD CHILD

ABOUT THE AUTHOR

Cindi Myers's idea of the perfect vacation is one spent whittling down her massive to-be-read pile. If warm sun, waves and handsome cabana boys to bring her drinks and food are also involved, that's even better. Cindi lives in the Colorado Mountains with her husband and two spoiled dogs.

Books by Cindi Myers

HARLEQUIN BLAZE
82—JUST 4 PLAY
118—RUMOR HAS IT
149—TAKING IT ALL OFF
168—GOOD, BAD...BETTER
180—DO ME RIGHT
215—ROCK MY WORLD*
241—NO REGRETS*
274—FEAR OF FALLING†
323—THE MAN TAMER
333—MEN AT WORK
  "Taking His Measure"

HARLEQUIN ANTHOLOGY
A WEDDING IN PARIS
  "Picture Perfect"

* The Wrong Bed
† It Was a Dark and Sexy Night...

**HARLEQUIN
AMERICAN ROMANCE**
1182—MARRIAGE ON
        HER MIND

HARLEQUIN NEXT
MY BACKWARDS LIFE
THE BIRDMAN'S DAUGHTER

**HARLEQUIN
SIGNATURE SELECT**
LEARNING CURVES
BOOTCAMP
  "Flirting with an Old Flame"

Don't miss any of our special offers. Write to us at the following address for information on our newest releases.

Harlequin Reader Service
U.S.: 3010 Walden Ave., P.O. Box 1325, Buffalo, NY 14269
Canadian: P.O. Box 609, Fort Erie, Ont. L2A 5X3

1

THE SAD TRUTH WAS, Sara Montgomery did not set out to be a corporate drone—one of those blue-suited types chained to a computer and cell phone. But somewhere between her wild-child past and her twenty-sixth birthday, that's exactly what she'd become. Even now, on vacation at a Malibu beach house, when she'd taken her pals Ellie and Candy's dare and vowed to leave work behind her for the week, she hadn't been able to leave her laptop at home.

"It's sick, I tell you," Candy Calder said as she watched Sara unpack the iBook. A diminutive brunette with violet eyes who worked at a software firm in the same office building as Sara and Ellie, Candy was the life of every party—an expert at leaving work at work. "You're supposed to be relaxing, not working."

"I only brought it to check e-mail," Sara said. "Just in case there's an emergency." Of course, with Uncle Spence, everything was an emergency. But what if he *really* needed her while she was away? "I'll only check it once a day."

"Come walking on the beach with us." The third

member of the group, Ellie Rockwell, a glam-goth chick who owned the coffee shop on the ground floor of their building, rubbed sunscreen on her arms, her long dark fingernails standing out against her pale skin. "It's a gorgeous day. I hear the surf's up and that means lots of beautiful bronzed bodies to admire."

Sara set the laptop on the table and stashed the case behind the sofa. "And of course, your walk will just *happen* to take you past a certain beach house not far from here where a certain good-looking man is staying?"

Candy blushed. "Ellie wants to say hello to her brother. There's nothing wrong with that." Ellie's brother, Matt, worked with Candy and was conveniently vacationing at a bungalow down the beach.

"And there's nothing wrong with you talking with a coworker." Sara grinned. "Maybe even flirting a little. I mean, that's one of the big reasons for this vacation, right? So that you can get the man you've been not-so-secretly lusting after?"

Candy rolled her eyes. "That is *not* why we're here. I'm going to prove to Matt—who is my *boss,* not my potential bed partner—that I can be serious about work. I'm not just a party girl."

"And *you're* on this vacation to learn how to loosen up," Ellie reminded Sara. "To forget about work for a while—" she eyed the laptop "—and have some fun. Find a gorgeous guy and get laid." Her eyes sparkled with laughter.

Sara ignored the tickle in her belly at the idea of

handsome men and sex—things that had been missing from her life for too long now. "I know why I'm here," she said. "And I promise, I am going to have fun. I just have to check in with the office...."

When the others raised their voices in protest, she changed the subject. "Let's not forget why Ellie is here," she said. "It's not only to look after the rest of us."

Ellie fluffed her dead-black locks and avoided looking either of them in the eye. "I'm here because I'm a big fan of *Sin on the Beach*. And I got us a great deal on the beach house...and I thought it would be fun."

"*And* you need to take a break from looking after everyone else and do something for you," Sara said.

Ellie nodded. "Right. And I intend to do that...as soon as I know that you two are all set for killer vacations on your own. Which means no computer for you—" she pointed to Sara "—and more time with my good-looking but lonely brother for you." She wagged a finger at Candy.

Candy made a face. "I know you have your heart set on the two of us hooking up, but honestly, Matt isn't interested in me that way. And I don't see him that way, either. I only want to impress him with my work skills."

Ellie's grin didn't fade. "I think you impress him all right," she said. "You just don't realize how much." She shouldered her beach bag. "Come on, let's go. And Sara—put away that laptop now. Before I hide the power cord."

"I'll relax as soon as I finish a few last-minute

details." Sara tried to ignore the guilt pinching at her. "I promised Uncle Spence." She'd log on for a few minutes, make sure no catastrophes had struck in the few hours she'd been away from the office, then she'd be free to enjoy the rest of the weekend.

"Your Uncle Spence is so nice," Ellie said. "He always leaves a tip for his double-shot espressos. I'm sure he'd understand if you didn't work on your vacation."

"Uncle Spence *is* a nice man." All the more reason not to let him down. She shooed her two friends toward the door. "You two go on. I promise I'll change into my swimsuit, take a quick look at my e-mail, then I'll catch up with you."

"All right then." Candy lingered in the doorway. "If you're going to be here for a few minutes longer, can you do me a favor?"

"Sure." Favors she could handle—obligations were the real bitches these days.

"Call me on my cell in a minute?"

"Okay. Any particular reason why?"

"Pretend you're a business colleague. But wait until we've had time to get to Matt's place. I want him to see that I *can* be serious about work."

"Even when you're on vacation?" She nodded, holding back a smile. "Gotcha." Apparently Candy didn't see the irony in pretending to do exactly what she'd lectured Sara against. Maybe because her fun-loving friend was a pro at mixing business and pleasure, while Sara had never been able to figure out how to juggle the two.

When they were out the door, Sara fished a brand-new bright-orange bikini from her suitcase and slipped it on. Her reflection in the bathroom mirror made her flinch. Her fish-belly white complexion was *not* a pretty sight. Why hadn't she thought to buy a bottle of fake bake when she was out shopping for the bikini? The glare off her white skin was liable to interfere with satellite transmission or something.

Grabbing a bottle of sunscreen and the laptop, she went out onto the beach house's broad veranda and settled into a cushioned lounge chair. At least here she could *see* the beach and enjoy the sound of waves crashing on the sand. Even if she was at her computer, lounging in a bikini with the ocean as a backdrop didn't exactly count as work, did it?

She looked down the shoreline for some sign of Candy and Ellie, but staggered rows of beach houses blocked her view of them. She'd give them a few more minutes to reach Matt's place before she called.

She signed on to her e-mail and waded through half a dozen spam messages, all promising extreme outcomes in the subject line. As if she needed increased anatomy or free designer knock-offs. When she spied a message marked with the word *Urgent!* she didn't even have to check the sender to know this was from Uncle Spence. Stomach fluttering with dread, she opened the e-mail and read through a message completely in caps and heavily punctuated with exclamation marks. Maybe she should ask Ellie to switch Spence to decaf.

While she was composing her reply, her cell

phone chirped. She retrieved it from her tote bag and checked the number. Frowning, she hit the answer button. "Hello, Uncle Spence."

"Sara, why haven't you answered my messages?" Spence's Southern gentleman's drawl was laced with tension. "I'm leaving for the golf course to play eighteen holes with Benton Granger. He's going to want to know about that deal you've been working on for him."

"Tell him everything's on schedule for his closing next Thursday." She logged off her e-mail.

"Are you sure? We haven't heard back from the title company yet, have we? And what about the survey?"

"The survey came in Friday. It's in the file. And the title company is supposed to call tomorrow."

"You should call them today." In the background she heard the hushed, reverent commentary of the Golf Channel announcers on TV. "If there's anything I've learned in my years in this business, it's that you have to stay on people to get them to complete tasks in a timely manner."

She rolled her eyes. Spence Montgomery's business philosophy in a nutshell: management by nagging. "Everything will be fine," she said. "Don't worry."

"It's my job to worry. And yours, too. It takes worry—and a great deal of hard work—to stay on top in this business. I'd have thought you'd have learned that from me, if nothing else."

She had learned it all right. Since she was seventeen and her uncle had given her a job as a clerk at his business, Anderson Title, he had taught her the importance of hard work. And she'd been a good pupil; once she'd graduated college, he'd promoted her and she'd taken on more and more responsibility every year. The business had blossomed into a multimillion-dollar concern, processing over a hundred mortgage loans a month.

Sara loved the business. And she loved Uncle Spence. She owed all her current success to him. But he really did worry too much. "When you see Mr. Granger, tell him everything is going great."

"It would be better if you were here to make sure of that."

"I'll be back in the office next week. I'll take care of his account then."

"I think you should call the title company today. Just to make sure they haven't run into any snags."

"Uncle Spence, I'm on vacation."

"One brief call won't make that much of a difference. And it would set Granger's mind at ease—and mine as well."

She checked her watch. It was a little after one o'clock. She could phone Marsha, then hit the beach. "Okay. I'll call. And I'll e-mail you to let you know everything's okay. But then I'm turning my phone off."

"Don't do that! What if I need you?"

There had been a time when she'd been flattered by Spence saying he needed her. But the warm fuzzies had worn off some time ago. "You've been in this business a lot longer than I have. I'm sure you can handle anything that comes up."

"You're responsible for your own clients, Sara. Remember, at Anderson Title we pride ourselves on our customer service." The implication that he would be disappointed if she provided anything less than the best hung heavy in the air.

She sighed. She couldn't say no to Uncle Spence. "All right. But please promise not to call me unless it's an emergency."

"That's my girl." The cheerfulness was back in his voice. "I promise. I don't know what I'd do without you."

"Goodbye. And don't worry." She might as well tell the waves to stop moving.

She checked her watch again. Candy and Ellie ought to have reached Matt's beach house by now. She punched in Candy's number. The line rang and rang, but there was no response. Odd. Maybe Candy was too involved in a conversation with Matt to answer.

Sara shrugged and set aside the phone, then clicked on the address book on her computer to retrieve Marsha's number. While she waited for the program to open, she stared out at the ocean.

A figure appeared on the horizon—the dark outline of a surfer against an expanse of blue sky and foaming white water. As she watched, he moved closer. She could tell it was a man now, broad-shouldered, wearing Hawaiian print board shorts.

She leaned forward, holding her breath as he rode

the crest of a perfect curl. Knees slightly bent, arms held a little apart from his body, he was precisely balanced on the board, a picture of grace and strength.

Her heart twisted with longing as she watched the man. Oh, to be able to tame the ocean that way. To have such command over the waves and your own body. When she was a girl, she'd spent a lot of time on the beach, mooning after various surfing gods. She'd never gotten farther than being "allowed" to hold surfboards while her crushes headed off with some other bikini-clad babe.

Of course she'd also been skipping school, experimenting with drugs and hanging out with the wrong crowd. She was one short step away from juvenile delinquency when her mother's brother, Spence, had reined her in.

But she hadn't been all bad in those days. She smiled, remembering. Sure, she'd been a little reckless. A little wild. But she'd also been fun and spontaneous. Words that didn't play a big part in her life these days.

Wasn't that part of the reason she'd come on this vacation—to get in touch with that inner wild child again? To rediscover the fun of being a little reckless?

She stood and leaned over the railing to watch the surfer more closely. He was tall and muscular, bronzed from hours in the sun. Exactly the kind of guy she'd panted after years ago.

Okay, so she could admit to herself that he was

the kind of guy who still made her feel a little out of breath. Just because she'd been too busy working these past few years to have time for a relationship with the opposite sex didn't mean she was dead.

That was the whole point of this vacation, wasn't it? She was here to prove to Ellie and Candy—and most importantly, to herself—that she still had what it took to have fun and really *live*.

She checked the surfer again. Great abs. Great legs. Great tan. Her lips curved in a smile. Exactly the kind of man she could go for.

So why not go for him? The idea sent a thrill of anticipation through her and she stood up straighter. What better way to wake up her dormant libido and rev up her inner party girl than a fling with a hot surfer?

The surfer rode the wave until it died in the shallows, then came ashore, pulling the board behind him by its leash. She couldn't tear her gaze away as he emerged from the water like some mythical sea god. Or maybe the star in one of her more vivid sexual fantasies…

"Hello!"

With a start, she realized he'd spotted her. He moved closer, waving.

She smiled and waved back, her heart galloping in her chest.

"Come on down! The waves are great!" he called.

She hesitated. Here was the opening she'd been looking for. "I'll be right there!" she called. She started toward the stairs leading down from the deck to the beach, hesitated, then did an about-face and grabbed the cell phone. Candy would give her a hard time if she saw, but what could Sara say? She wasn't ready to go cold turkey yet. Besides, it wasn't as if she expected another call or anything. She just felt kind of…naked…without it.

DREW LEANED his board against the deck pilings and waited for the young woman to join him. She was wearing a bright-orange bikini that showed off her very sexy curves. He was glad she'd agreed to join him. When he'd spotted her she'd been watching him with a wistful look on her face. As if she really didn't want to be on that deck by herself.

Since he'd started off the day feeling lonely himself, he figured maybe the two of them could help each other out. And it didn't hurt that she looked hot in that bikini. "Hi, I'm Drew Jamison." He stood at the top of the steps and held out his hand. "Welcome to Malibu."

"Hello. I'm Sara." She hesitated, then stepped forward and took his hand. She had a firm, business-like grip, but her hand was cold. He cupped it in his and rubbed back and forth. "You ought to get out into the sun and warm up."

She pulled away and turned to look out over the ocean, her cheeks a becoming pink. Obviously, she wasn't used to strangers rubbing her hand. *Way to go, Drew,* he thought. *Scare her off, first thing.*

He struck a casual pose next to his board, pretending to look out at the waves while watching her out of the corner of his eye. He kept a good three feet of space between them. He didn't want her to think he was the type to come on too strong.

"How long have you been surfing?"

Her voice was soft, with a slight Southern drawl that sent heat through him that had nothing to do with the Malibu sun. "I've been doing it since I was a kid," he said. "Almost twenty-five years."

"You're very good." She glanced at him, a shy smile transforming her face.

There went another heat wave. If she was flirting with him she was keeping it low key, but his body was responding as if she'd turned on the charm one hundred percent. Guess he was lonelier than he'd thought. He grinned. "Thanks. I run the surf shop down the way, the Surf Shack. My grandpa owns the place, so I've been hanging out there for years. I give lessons too, if you're interested in learning how to surf while you're here."

Her smile brightened. "I'd like that. Though we only have the cottage for a week."

His grin evaporated. "We?" Just his luck, she had a burly boyfriend or husband lurking somewhere.

"I'm here with two girlfriends. We came down from L.A. for a few days' break."

Ah. Two *friends*. That sounded better. "Where are you from originally?" he asked. "That doesn't sound like an L.A. accent."

She laughed. "No, that always gives me away." She faced him. "I'm originally from Georgia. I moved here with my mom when I was in high school, after my dad died. Her brother—my Uncle

Spence—was living in L.A. and he sort of helped her raise me. What about you? Are you a native?"

"Yep. Lived here all my life."

"No wonder you're such a good surfer."

He shrugged. "I don't do it as much as I'd like. Running a business takes a lot of time. That and family obligations."

"Don't I know it." She motioned to the phone in her other hand. "I can't even get away from the business when I'm on vacation. And my Uncle Spence, bless his heart, expects me to do everything."

"Then it sounds to me like you really *need* a vacation." He moved closer. "And I'd really love some company this afternoon."

The thought of going back into the water, or back to work, by himself held no appeal now that he'd met Sara. If she was only going to be here a week, he didn't want to waste any time getting to know her better.

She looked out at the waves again. "I'll admit it's tempting." She glanced back at her phone. "I could always finish my work later…."

He was congratulating himself on saying the right thing when her phone rang. He silently willed her not to answer it, but he had the feeling she wasn't the type to ignore a ringing phone.

She gave him an apologetic look then took the call. "Hello? Oh, hi, Candy. Are you at Matt's already?"

He walked a short distance away so she'd have a little privacy and tried not to listen to the "uh-huhs" and "oh reallys" that punctuated her half of the conversation. He hoped she didn't get sidetracked by work and decide she couldn't come with him.

Timing was everything, in surfing as well as life. Five years ago, his grandfather, Gus, had suffered a massive heart attack. He'd recovered, but last year a second coronary had laid him low. He'd been in danger of losing the Surf Shack when Drew had stepped in to help. He'd been behind the counter at the Shack ever since, while Gus helped out as he could. Now that his doctors had declared surfing off-limits, Gus mostly played the role of local surfing "character," sharing stories of his heyday as a surfing king to anyone who cared to hang around.

Drew hadn't really minded returning to the place where he'd grown up, but between living with his grandfather and running the Surf Shack, surfing was something he could never get away from. He loved it, but he felt pressured by it, too. Last night after Gus was in bed, Drew had stayed up to balance the Shack accounts. Midway through reviewing inventory records, he'd realized this was no way for a twenty-nine-year-old guy to spend Sunday night.

The sudden loneliness had hit him in the gut, and this morning he'd vowed to change things. He'd get out more, meet women and find someone to share his life with.

So was it mere coincidence that the first woman he'd met seemed to want the same thing for herself? Maybe he was reading too much into a wistful look and a few words of conversation, but something in him sensed that Sara was a woman who wanted more.

Maybe he could be the one to give her what she wanted.

"Sorry about that." She walked up behind him, tote bag slung over her shoulder. "I was afraid that would be my Uncle Spence calling with some urgent business problem, but it was just one of my roommates."

"So you're free to come with me now?"

She smiled. "I'm free. At least for a little while. And I'd better take advantage of that."

2

THE COOL firmness of sand between her toes, the smell of salt and suntan oil, the thunder of waves and the shrill cries of seagulls transported Sara to her girlhood. Walking alongside Drew, she felt that same sense of possibility to the afternoon—that wonderful anticipation she'd come to Malibu to rediscover. With a surfboard tucked under one arm, he even *looked* like the idols of her youth. Anything could happen as long as the sun shone and her companion kept smiling at her.

She glanced at him and he winked. Now she *really* felt like a girl again; it was all she could do not to giggle. She was glad she'd agreed to come with him. He was easy to be with, and he'd given her the perfect excuse to get away, though her phone was in the beach bag she'd grabbed to bring along.

Whether she could go through with her original plan to seduce this hottie was debatable. Her seduction skills were definitely rusty.

Ellie would probably say that was all the more reason for her to practice.

They passed a carnival laid out on the sand—

Ferris wheel, arcade games, a stage and volleyball nets. A man in a lime-green turban and a Hawaiian shirt stood at a booth near a sign that read Magellan the All-Knowing. "What's all this?" Sara asked.

"It's all part of the big *Sin on the Beach* party." Drew raised one eyebrow. "I figured that was what brought you here this week."

She shrugged. "My friends said something about it, but I never realized it was so…elaborate."

He nodded. "They're hosting a week-long bash— games, dancing, contests, prizes. It's bigger than spring break."

A week-long bash? "Guess we lucked out." She grinned at him. Talk about the perfect setting for a wild fling.

"My shop is just a little ways up the beach," Drew said. "My grandparents started it almost forty years ago."

"It's hard to imagine having a grandfather who surfs," she said. "It seems like such a hip, young thing to do." Her own mother—like her father before he'd died—was a serious, hard-working person. Even after they'd moved to L.A., her mom had never acclimated to the west-coast lifestyle. She complained that the sun shone too much.

"Grandpa Gus definitely isn't an old fogey," Drew said. "If anything, he acts too young. He forgets he can't do everything he could as a young man and it gets him into trouble."

"And you worry about him," she said.

He gave her a sharp look. "Does it show that much?"

"Not really. But I can relate. I'm the same way with my Uncle Spence. He's younger than your grandfather, but he works so hard. He never lets himself relax, and he worries about everything. He depends on me a lot to help with his business and I hate to let him down."

Drew nodded. "I love Grandpa, and I don't really mind, but sometimes…" His voice trailed away.

"Yeah, sometimes." She knew exactly how Drew felt. Could it be she wasn't the only young adult in the world with too many responsibilities and too much guilt?

"Would you like to see the shop?" Drew asked. "Then maybe we could do something together."

She could think of any number of things she would like to do with him—some of which involved wearing no clothes. Obviously her libido was taking the idea of a no-holds-barred vacation seriously. But even the more sensible part of her liked the idea of getting to know this man better. "That would be great," she said.

Like a bad-tempered chaperone determined to cramp her style, her phone started vibrating, rattling against the keys in the bottom of her bag.

"What is that?" Drew asked.

"Nothing." She groped in her bag, trying to locate the off button for the phone, but only succeeded in getting the strap wrapped around her sunglasses case.

"Seriously, what's that buzzing noise?" Drew moved closer. "Do you have something in there?"

"No, really, it's fine." If she broke off yet another conversation with him to take a call, he was going to think she was a complete workaholic.

He stepped back, grinning. "I've heard about those things, but I never knew a woman who carried one with her to the beach."

"It's not… You don't think—" Her face probably came close to matching the color of her swimsuit. She jerked the cell out of her bag. "It's a phone!"

He laughed. "Hey, did I say it wasn't?" He shook his head. "Go ahead and answer it. Maybe it's your roommate again."

She should be so lucky. She checked the caller ID. "No, it's my uncle."

"Then you'd better answer it."

"Yeah, guess I'd better." She flipped open the phone as she moved a few steps away.

"Sara, why haven't you called the title company?" With those words, Uncle Spence made her magical mood vanish.

The title company! She groaned. "I'm sorry. I got busy and it slipped my mind. I'll call in the morning."

"You need to call now. Granger's been asking me about the closing." She pictured him standing in the clubhouse, sweat pouring down his red face, working himself into a lather over his imagined failure to make a good impression on his top client. "We're having dinner later and I'd like to be able to tell him something specific," he said.

"Just tell Mr. Granger that everything's on schedule and he doesn't need to worry."

"Do you have that flow chart you made up that shows the closing process and everything that happens?"

"Ye-es." She glanced at Drew. He was leaning on his board, looking out at the ocean. She hoped he wasn't getting impatient.

"I'll give you a number to fax it to," Spence said. "I'll give it to Granger at dinner. He's wild for any kind of chart or graph."

"I don't have a fax machine right here."

"Then e-mail it to the office. I'll have Tabitha print it out and fax it."

Drew glanced over at her. She waved. "Uncle Spence, can't this wait?" she asked. "I'm really busy with something else right now."

"How long will it take you to e-mail that chart? And one call to the title company isn't so much to ask." He sighed, sounding sad. "I'm really counting on you, Sara. It's not like you to let me down."

Every word was like another bucketful of sand being poured over her, burying her in guilt. She swallowed hard. "Okay. I'll see what I can do."

She hung up. So much for a carefree afternoon of romance. "Is something wrong?" Drew returned to her side. "You look upset."

"I'm sorry, I have to go," she said. She replaced the phone in her bag, avoiding his eyes. "Something's come up at the office…I'm sorry."

"You can't let someone else take care of it?" he asked.

She shook her head. "No. I'd better go."

She could feel his gaze on her, intense and probing, and disappointment dragged at her. He was such a great guy. They could have had fun together…. She shook her head. "It was great meeting you," she said. Lame words, full of regret for what might have been.

"Yeah. Maybe I'll see you around."

"Yeah." Except she'd be too mortified to go anywhere near him again.

Surfboard tucked under his arm, he strode across the sand. She watched him go, suppressing a sigh. Drew was just too perfect. She'd blown it. Lost her chance. She was doomed to a life chained to her computer.

HALF AN HOUR later, Sara had just finished e-mailing the flow chart to Uncle Spence and was debating opening a bottle of wine for her own private pity party when Ellie ran into the beach house. She skidded to a stop and her smile vanished when she saw Sara hunched over the computer. "Hey, what are you doing still working?" she said. "You promised to put that thing away."

"I did put it away," Sara said, shutting the lid to the laptop and turning to her friend. "I even went for a walk on the beach."

"That's more like it." Ellie dropped onto the sofa. "So…did you meet any hot guys?"

Sara felt her face warm. "There was this one surfer…."

"I knew it!" Ellie leaned forward, hands between her knees. "What happened? Did you talk to him?

Did he think you were hot? Did you tell him you needed someone to help you relax? Did you suggest going somewhere and having wild monkey sex?"

Sara laughed at the onslaught of questions. Leave it to Ellie to put her in a better mood. "I talked to him," she said. "His name is Drew, and he runs a local surf shop."

"Drew." Ellie tried the name on her tongue. "Mmm. And is Drew dreamy? Or delicious?" She smiled wickedly.

Heat curled through Sara at the memory of Drew's bronzed muscles and killer smile. "Both. And he was really nice, too."

"Then what are you doing sitting around here by yourself?"

Gloom engulfed Sara once more. "Everything was going great, then Uncle Spence called."

"Sara!" Ellie clenched her hands. "Why did you answer the phone?"

"I wasn't going to," Sara said. "But Drew told me I should." She winced at the memory. He had been so considerate. So understanding.

"What did Spence want?" Ellie asked.

"He wanted some information for a client he's having dinner with tonight."

"Then he should have gotten it himself," Ellie said. "You should have told him so."

Sara nodded. "I know. I tell myself I'm going to stand up to him, but whenever I balk at what he wants, he plays the guilt card." She shrugged. "It's easier just to do the work and not have to deal with the guilt."

Ellie patted Sara's hand. "I know, hon. Spence depends on you for so much. Too much. And you have a soft heart."

And a soft head, Sara thought.

"So you came back here to get the information for Uncle Spence," Ellie said. "You should've invited surfer boy back with you."

Sara raised her head. "I never even thought of that. After Uncle Spence's call it seemed like the mood had been destroyed."

"Do you think Drew was angry about what happened?" Ellie asked.

"No. He was really nice about it. I just felt bad." She'd wanted a hole in the sand to open up and swallow her. What woman in her right mind would forsake a gorgeous guy in favor of more work?

Ellie sat back, her expression thoughtful. "You say he runs a surf shop?"

Sara nodded. "It's called the Surf Shack. His grandfather owns it."

Ellie grinned. "That's perfect." She snatched the *Sin on the Beach* flyer from the coffee table. "There's a surfing competition as part of the festival. You used to surf, right?"

"I hung out with surfers, but I never learned myself." Back then her focus had been more on the hot guys and the beach-bunny lifestyle than on surfing itself. Now she wished she *had* taken advantage of the opportunity to learn. "That was a long time ago."

"Then it's time you learned how." Ellie handed her the flyer. "Tomorrow morning, you'll go down to the Surf Shack and sign up for the tournament. And you'll tell Drew you want a private lesson from him."

Ellie made things sound so simple. "What if he says no?" Sara asked.

"You wear that orange bikini and a big smile and I guarantee he won't say no." She patted Sara's hand again. "Come on. A woman who can handle million-dollar real estate transactions ought to be able to persuade a guy she likes to spend time with her."

Sara nodded, still unsure, but she was determined to overcome her doubts. She was tired of being a by-stander in life, and never a participant. If she didn't do something, she was going to waste the best years of her life working all the time and end up alone. "Okay," she said. "Tomorrow I'll do it. But let's not talk about it anymore." She didn't want to risk talking herself right out of this crazy idea. "I want to hear what you did today. How did it go with Matt and Candy?"

"When I left the two of them Candy was playing nose-to-the-grindstone—going on about work and some computer presentation and needing his input. Matt was looking as if he didn't know what hit him." Ellie grinned. "If Candy would only open her eyes and really *look* at my brother, she'd realize how crazy he is about her. I mean, come on—she's every red-blooded man's dream babe. But she's so convinced he sees her as an airhead. She can't believe he might be interested."

And Ellie obviously couldn't see that she might

be a *little* prejudiced in her brother's favor. "Matt is a great guy," Sara said. "And of course you love him. But maybe he's too serious for a woman like Candy. The girl does like to party."

Ellie shook her head. "I have a sense for these kinds of things. I have a feeling this vacation is going to be very good for Matt and Candy."

It was just like Ellie to always be worrying about others' problems. She'd turned her coffee shop, Dark Gothic Roast, into therapy central for their office complex. But what did Ellie want? "What did you do after you left Candy and Matt?" Sara asked.

"I walked along the beach and checked out all the stuff set up for the festival. There's a huge carnival, all kinds of games and attractions and the film set where they're going to be taping a special episode of the show." She squirmed and glanced at Sara out of the corner of her eye. "They're even going to be auditioning for extras tomorrow morning."

"That's awesome," Sara said. "You should try out." She didn't know anyone who was a bigger fan of *Sin on the Beach* than Ellie, and though she probably would never have admitted it, Sara sensed an inner diva in her friend dying to get out.

"Oh, I could never do that," Ellie protested. She glanced down at her black shorts and shirt. "I don't exactly have the *Sin on the Beach* style they're looking for."

"So we give you the style," Sara said. "You've got a gorgeous figure. You're young and hip. All you need is to lighten your hair a little, add a little color to your wardrobe and voila! Instant beach babe."

Ellie looked doubtful. "I don't know…."

"You know you want to do this," Sara said.

"Yes, but… There is one other problem."

"What is it?"

"I know the director."

"That's great!" She studied Ellie's pained expression. "Isn't it?"

Ellie shrugged. "His name's Bill. We were next-door neighbors when I was a kid. I doubt if he even remembers me."

Something in Ellie's expression helped Sara read between the lines. "But you remember him," she said.

Ellie nodded. "I had a huge crush on him back then." She paused, then added, "When I saw him today, it was as if nothing had changed." She smiled. "He is *so* hot, and he has this awesome tattoo."

Sara laughed. Ellie had a thing for guys with tattoos. "This gets better and better," she said.

"What do you mean *better?*" Ellie said. "I can't think of anything worse than blowing it in front of my old crush."

"Who says you're going to blow it?" Sara said. "And I'm not so convinced he doesn't remember you. You're not exactly an easy woman to forget."

"I was just a kid," Ellie said. "Nothing like I am now."

"All the more reason to show him how grown-up you are," Sara said. "Think about it. Candy and Matt are bound to end up with something going on this trip. You've convinced me to see how far I can get with Drew. Now you need to go forward with Bill."

Ellie grinned. "When you put it that way... I mean, I wouldn't want to let the two of you down."

"That's the spirit. If I can work up the nerve to sign up for surfing lessons, then you can find the courage to go to that audition."

Their eyes met and Ellie nodded. "Okay, it's a deal."

They clasped hands. "Beach babes unite," Sara said.

"The men won't know what hit them," Ellie echoed. "This is going to be the best vacation ever."

DREW COUNTED the last of the change in the register and shut the drawer with a bang. Time to start another day in the salt mines. Of course, running a surf shop wasn't the same as hard labor, but it wasn't the carefree surfing lifestyle he'd once enjoyed. His conversation with Sara yesterday afternoon had reminded him how much was missing in his life.

And in hers, too, by the sound of things. Too bad she'd had to leave when she did. Of course, he knew where to find her, but maybe it was better to end things before they started. For all they had in common, neither one of them seemed to have room in their lives for a relationship.

"What are you so glum about?" Gus spoke from his customary place on a stool at the end of the front counter. Dressed in red board shorts and a worn T-shirt that proclaimed Surfers Stay on Longer, Gus still wore the long sideburns and handlebar mustache that had been his trademark in his surfing days, though his hair was now white instead of blond. Seventy years and two heart attacks had hardly slowed him down. If anything, Gus seemed more determined than ever to go at life full tilt.

Between the stress of managing a booming business and worries about Gus overdoing it, it was a wonder Drew slept at all. "I've got a lot on my mind, that's all," he said.

"You're too young to be such a sad sack," Gus said. "You need to get out and have some fun." He picked up a bright-orange flyer from a stack at the end of the counter. "This *Sin on the Beach* festival has all kinds of things you could get involved in." He took a pair of glasses from his shirt pocket and put them on, then read from the flyer. "There's limbo dancing, a pool tournament, volleyball, body painting—hmm, now that sounds interesting. Oh, and look—surfing." He grinned at Drew over the edge of the paper. "It says here the surfing competition is sponsored by Beach Babe Bronzer and the Surf Shack. Guess that means you're disqualified from entering."

"Guess so," Drew said. He'd signed up months ago to sponsor the contest, thinking it would be good publicity. Everyone who wanted to enter the competition had to sign up in person at the Surf Shack, and he was offering special deals on equipment rental and lessons.

"Just as well." Gus laid aside the paper and took

off his glasses. "I hear the judge for the contest is really tough. Some former surfing champion or something."

"Is that right?" Drew grinned. "I hear he's just some old geezer."

Gus joined in Drew's laughter. "I may be old, but I can still out-surf three quarters of the young dudes on this beach," he said.

"Maybe so." Drew's expression sobered. "But you don't have to prove anything to them. Remember what the doctor said."

"Doctors!" Gus's voice was filled with scorn. "They may know a lot about medicine, but what do they know about living? The only reason I'm in as good a shape as I am at my age is because I've stayed active. How many of those doctors do you think could hang ten on a monster curl? I could do it with my eyes closed."

Drew knew the old man was telling the truth. Back in the day, Gus Jamison had been a three-time world surfing champion. Two generations of surfers had learned to shred waves under his tutelage. But his heart attacks had ended all that—if only Drew could get his grandfather to accept it.

He picked up the clipboard that held the entry forms for the surfing competition and ruffled through the papers. "You're not going to have time for surfing anyway," he said. "I expect we're going to be really busy during this festival. I'll need your help here in the shop."

"Sure, I'll help out as much as I can," Gus said.

"But I'm going to be spending some time down at the *Sin on the Beach* set."

Drew had a good idea why his grandfather might be attracted to the television production. Gus might be seventy, but he still had an appreciation for pretty women in bikinis. "What business do you have down there?" Drew asked. "Are you hoping one of those actresses will need help with her wardrobe?"

Gus sat up straighter. "For your information, I've been hired for a role in the series."

All the breath rushed out of Drew and he stared at his grandfather. "What?"

"Some producer from the show came in here yesterday afternoon while you were out. He was looking for props to use on the set. We got to talking and the next thing I knew he asked if I'd be interested in a small part in the episode they're filming." Gus stroked his mustache. "I guess he recognized star quality when he saw it."

Drew shook his head. "Grandpa, you never cease to amaze me."

"It's called charisma, boy. I like to think I passed some of it on to you." He arched one eyebrow. "I understand the show is auditioning for extras this morning. Maybe you ought to go down there and try out."

"I think one star in the family is enough," Drew said. "Besides, somebody has to stay here and run the shop."

"You worry too much about this business," Gus said. "It's a surf shop, not IBM. Cooter can keep an eye on things if we're not here."

Drew nodded. The Surf Shack's sole employee, Cooter Dixon, was an affable beach bum who knew almost as much about surfing as Drew and Gus. He was capable enough, but it wasn't the same as having one of the shop's owners behind the front counter.

"I want you to get out there and have some fun for a change," Gus said. He picked up a flier and perched his glasses on his nose once more. "It says here, participants can earn points and a chance to win a beach house."

"I already have a beach house," Drew said. "Why would I need another one?"

Gus scowled at him. "Do I have to teach you everything? Find some sexy beach bunny and offer to help *her* win points toward the beach house."

An image of Sara wearing that hot bikini popped into Drew's mind. He wouldn't mind some fun and games with her. Then his daydream morphed as a cell phone appeared in Sara's hand. He frowned. It figured that the first woman he'd been really attracted to in ages was even more distracted by work and responsibility than he was.

"I'll make a deal with you," Gus said.

Drew eyed his grandfather warily. "What kind of deal?"

"You sign up to participate in some of these festival activities and I promise to behave myself and take it easy."

"When have you ever behaved yourself?" Drew said.

Gus grinned. "They say even an old dog can learn new tricks."

"Let me see that flyer." He held out his hand and Gus passed him one of the brightly colored sheets of paper. He scanned the list of activities at the bottom. He had to admit some of them sounded like fun. It had been a long time—almost the entire two years he'd run the shop—since he'd cut loose. It might do him good to relax a little. And if he could convince a certain babe in an orange bikini to relax with him… He grinned. Then Gus might not be the only ladies' man in the family.

3

SARA CLUTCHED her beach bag more tightly to her side and fought the urge to turn around. Ellie had kept her part of their bargain and headed out bright and early this morning to the auditions for *Sin on the Beach.* After her makeover she'd looked fantastic— a little softer, but still sexy and just edgy enough to heat any man's blood. Unless this Bill guy was blind or gay, he wasn't going to be able to resist Ellie's combination of sex and savvy.

Now it was Sara's turn to master her nerves and sign up for the surfing tournament—and finagle a private lesson from Drew. She'd resolutely switched off her phone after sending an e-mail to Uncle Spence letting him know she'd be out of touch all day.

She did have her phone with her, strictly for emergencies, but it would stay in her bag and off unless absolutely necessary.

A leisurely walk down the beach from her bungalow brought her to the Surf Shack. The weathered building was perched on pilings just beyond the pier, with steps leading up to a broad front porch.

Sara stood out front for a moment, gathering her courage.

"Come on up, young lady." A stocky, white-haired man with a thick moustache, dressed in board shorts and a T-shirt came out onto the porch and beckoned to her. "Whatever it is you need, I can fix you right up."

She smiled and started up the steps. "Are you Gus?" she asked.

"I see my reputation precedes me." His grin broadened and he took her hand. "And what's your name?"

"Sara."

"It's a pleasure to meet you, Sara." His gaze swept over her appreciatively. "A pleasure indeed. Are you a surfer?"

She shook her head. "No. But I'd like to be."

"Then you've come to the right place." He started to lead her inside, then stopped and looked back at her. "Are you dating a surfer? Or anyone else?"

Amused by this odd line of questioning, she shook her head. "No."

"Perfect. Come inside. I want you to meet someone."

She allowed him to lead her inside, where Drew was busy at the front counter with a customer. He looked every bit as gorgeous this morning as she remembered—sun-bleached hair falling over his forehead, a faded T-shirt stretched across strong shoulders.

Not wanting to be caught staring at him, she looked around the shop. The place was packed with stacks of yellow and green life jackets, kneeboards, surfboards, shelves of sunblock, T-shirts, board shorts and surfing accessories. A giant plastic shark grinned from the wall above the cash register and a poster next to it advertised the Original Sex Wax.

The wall next to the door was devoted to photographs. Sara recognized a younger Gus—with blond hair—posing with a surfboard and a three-foot-tall gold trophy. In another photo, Gus stood with a younger couple and a little boy—Drew? She smiled and found the boy at various ages in other photos. High in one corner she found a more recent picture of Drew and his grandfather behind the counter at the Surf Shack.

Gus cleared his throat and Sara turned to find Drew staring at her. "Sara!" A smile spread across his face.

The sheer pleasure in his eyes left her weak-kneed. "Hi, Drew," she said.

"You two know each other?" Gus asked.

"We met yesterday afternoon." Drew approached her. "It's good to see you," he said.

"It's good to see you, too." She struggled to talk normally around the crazy fluttering in her chest. "I wanted to apologize for running off like that yesterday."

"It's okay. You had things you had to take care of."

He had the most beautiful brown eyes, with little flecks of gold in them. "I was hoping…maybe we could try again."

She was so mesmerized by Drew's proximity, so lost in his eyes, that she forgot all about Gus. Until he cleared his throat again and she jumped.

"Why don't you let me look after the shop this morning," Gus said. "You two go on and enjoy yourselves." He glanced out the window toward the beach and the sparkling ocean beyond. "It's a beautiful day out."

Drew frowned. "I don't know, Grandpa. People will be signing up for the tournament and lessons. It could get really busy."

"Cooter can help me. And it won't kill people if they have to wait their turn."

"I almost forgot," Sara said. "I have to sign up for the tournament."

"I thought you said you didn't surf," Drew said.

She fought back a blush. "I don't. But I've always wanted to learn." She shrugged. "The tournament seemed like a good incentive. Besides, you get points for entering, don't you?"

"You mean for the *Sin on the Beach* contest?" Drew picked up a clipboard from the counter and glanced at the papers clipped there. "It says here you get fifty points for entering."

"Great. My friends and I are trying to win the time share at the beach house."

Drew grunted as Gus elbowed him in the side. He frowned at his grandfather, then turned back to Sara. "There are a lot of activities this week for the festival—contests and stuff. Since the Surf Shack is one of the event sponsors, I'm not eligible to earn points for myself, but I could be a part of your team."

"That would be great." It would give them an excuse to spend more time together. "To tell you the truth, I was starting to worry I wouldn't be able to contribute enough to the group. My roommate Candy has already racked up a bunch of points. And my other roommate, Ellie, is trying out as an extra for *Sin on the Beach*. If she gets a part, she wins a ton of points."

"Your roommate wants to be on the show?" Gus interrupted them. "I have a part, you know."

"You do?" She tried to hide her surprise. Aging surfers didn't exactly fit the glamorous, sexy image usually associated with the hit show.

"I'm the crusty-but-lovable owner of the surf shop where the series stars keep their boards," Gus said. "Local color and all that."

"All Grandpa has to do is be himself," Drew said. He handed Sara the clipboard. "Fill out one of these forms and you'll be signed up for the tournament." He moved behind the counter and consulted an open spiral notebook. "Where's Cooter?" he asked.

"Out back," Gus said, "repairing a board."

Drew nodded and motioned to Sara. "When you're done with that, come out back with me and we'll fix you up with a board."

She returned the completed form, then followed him down a set of stairs, into a yard surrounded by high wooden privacy fencing. Except for narrow paths through the clutter, the space was crammed with rows of upright surfboards in various conditions, more life jackets, a trio of ocean kayaks and what appeared to be the back half of a '57 Chevy.

To the left of the stairs, a tall, wiry-haired young man

was melting wax over the bottom of a surfboard resting on a pair of wooden sawhorses. He looked up as they approached. "Hey dude," he said. He nodded to Sara.

"Sara, this is Cooter. Cooter, Sara." Drew made the introductions. "Sara needs a board."

"Give her one of those over there." Cooter gestured to a row of blue-and-white surfboards against the fence. "They're super sweet."

Drew stepped over a heap of life jackets and pulled out a board. "Find a life jacket that fits," he called over his shoulder.

She fished out a bright green jacket and followed him to a gate that gave access onto the beach. "Tell me about Gus," she said. "You said yesterday he'd had a heart attack?"

"Two." He held the gate open for her. "He was running the Surf Shack pretty much by himself and it was too much for him."

"So you stepped in to help."

He followed her along the side of the building. "My parents used to run it with him when I was a kid, but they retired to Arizona a few years ago and ended up opening a rock shop there." He shook his head. "They couldn't stand not working, but now they're so involved with that business, they couldn't leave it to help Grandpa."

"He's lucky to have you, then."

"It beats sitting behind a desk in an insurance office, which is what I was doing before."

"Still, it's a lot of responsibility." Not to mention how much he must worry about his grandfather.

He shrugged. "I try not to let it cramp my style." The smile he flashed made her feel a little light-headed. The word *devastating* came to mind. She hoped she wasn't out of her league here. After all, she hadn't had much practice at this relationship stuff.

When they reached the front of the building, he handed her the board and went to retrieve his own. "Do you have plenty of sunblock?" he asked when he joined her again.

"I do." Ellie had lectured them all on the danger of skin cancer. Her own goth-white skin testified to her devotion to SPF.

She left her beach bag in Gus's care, then headed down the shore with Drew. The sand was already strewn with beach chairs and vacationers sunning themselves on towels or reclining beneath umbrellas. Children splashed in the shallows while older teens and adults floated on the waves farther out. The smells of coconut suntan oil and salty seawater mingled with the polished-floor scent of the surfboards they carried.

"What beach did you hang out at when you were a kid?" Drew asked. "Was it this one?"

"Not usually. Most of the time I hung out at County Line Beach." In those days there hadn't been much at County Line but a few portable toilets and lots of surfers. It was the perfect place for anyone looking to get away from parents, school or too many rules. The perfect place for a kid to get into trouble, and Sara had found her share of that. She skipped school so much she almost failed her junior year of high school. She smoked pot, drank beer and wasn't above stealing snacks and small items from local stores on her way to the beach. The people she hung out with then were just like her—rebels and drop-outs who were truly at home only on the beach.

She wondered if things had changed much at her old hang-out. She hadn't been back in years.

"Good surfing there," Drew said. "Good diving at the kelp beds, too."

"Mostly I just hung out," she said. "Worked on my tan and watched the surfers." The guys and gals who rode the waves on longboards had represented the ultimate freedom to her. They were popular, tanned and at home in their environment in a way she—an awkward, fatherless teen who'd moved halfway across the country to a city where she knew no one— found difficult.

"Now you're going to *be* one of those surfers."

They walked past the crowds to an area of the shore that was almost deserted at this hour. "This is a good place to put in." Drew stopped and planted the tail of his board in the sand. "You want to start out with some small waves—stuff you won't even think worth surfing later."

She squinted out at the waves. They didn't look very large from here, but her stomach still fluttered with nervousness at the idea of trying to ride them. "I guess that's why no one else is here," she said.

"That's good. You want to avoid crowds. Plus, surfers get ticked off at beginners who get in their way."

"I think that's why I never learned before," she said. "I didn't want to be one of those people my heroes always complained about."

He laughed. "I've been one of those guys complaining myself, but I won't give you any grief today. We'll take it slow and before you know it, you'll be riding a wave. I promise."

She nodded, though she had her doubts. Still, she would never learn if she didn't try. This vacation was all about breaking out of old patterns and trying new things. "Okay. Where do we start?"

"First, we're going to do some push-ups."

"Push-ups?" She frowned at him. "You're going to make me work out before we get in the water?"

"We just need to practice a few moves that you'll use out there and it's easier to start on land."

She was still skeptical. "Push-ups?"

"Sort of. Watch me." He lay on his stomach in the sand. Dressed only in baggy Hawaiian print shorts, his body was brown and muscular, his legs long, dusted with golden hairs. Sara felt a tickle of desire in her midsection, and had a fleeting image of her lying in the sand beside him, rolling into his arms.

In one swift movement, he levered himself into a push-up, then sprang to a crouch, one foot in front of the other. He lifted his arms and balanced there, swaying slightly like a surfer adjusting his stance to the waves. He looked up at her and grinned. "Think you can do that?"

"Sure." She lay in the sand, trying to recall exactly what he'd done. She wasn't a gym rat, but she took the occasional yoga class and walked a lot around her neighborhood. That counted for exercise, didn't it?

"Now imagine you're on your board," Drew said. "A wave is coming. Jump up and ride it."

Hoisting her body into a push-up was no problem, but jumping into a crouch from there was more difficult than it had appeared. She wobbled into position, arms out, sand sticking to her chest and stomach.

"You need to move faster," Drew said. "Remember, that wave's coming and you have to get on your feet."

She tried again. "How's that?"

"Your feet need to be farther apart. The front foot should be near the middle of the board, sort of centered under your body, and the back foot should be toward the tail."

She tried again, and again, until she was panting and sweating. She looked up at Drew through a fringe of hair that had fallen into her eyes. "How's that?"

He nodded. "Better. You'll want to practice more on your own." He extended his hand and she took it. He pulled her to her feet and began brushing sand from her stomach and sides.

His hands were warm, and the contact made her warmer still. When his fingers grazed her breast a tremor shuddered through her and she swayed a little. He stilled and their eyes met, his gaze heated and intense. "Sorry," he mumbled.

"Don't be sorry." She wet her lips, hoping he'd

kiss her. Her mouth tingled in anticipation of his touch. Who cared about surfing? There were better things to do on a deserted section of beach.

But he looked away, and the moment passed. "I think we're ready to get in the water. First, attach your leash. That will keep you from losing your board when you fall off."

"Who says I'm going to fall off?" she teased as she snapped the tether around her ankle.

"You'll fall off. You won't learn if you don't." He straightened. "We're going to lie down on our boards and paddle out into the water."

"Sounds simple enough." She followed him out into the water, pushing her surfboard along in front of her.

"It's harder than it looks. Now get on your board."

She wrestled the surfboard into position and managed to flop down onto it—not an easy feat in the choppy water. "What now?"

"The most important thing is to balance. That's the key to surfing every step of the way. Keep your weight centered on the board. Don't lean back toward the tail. Paddle with cupped hands." He demonstrated and she mimicked him. They began to move forward, bobbing in the waves.

"This isn't bad." She grinned at him. "It's even kind of f—" At that moment, a larger wave descended, flipping her over. She came up sputtering, eyes stinging from the salt water.

"You okay?" Drew called.

"Fine." Everything except her dignity. She hoisted herself back onto her board.

Drew paddled over to her. "It's hard to paddle over bigger waves, so you need to learn to duck dive."

"Duck dive? As in going under water?" She didn't like the sound of that.

"Just for a minute. Just under the wave, really. It can be fun." He turned to study the horizon, then pointed. "See that bigger swell heading toward us?"

"I see it."

"Okay, you want to line up perpendicular to it, then a couple of feet before it reaches you, grab both sides of the board and shove the nose down. Once the nose is under, use your knee to force the tail under. Do it right and you'll bob right up on the other side of the wave."

"And if I do it wrong?"

He laughed. "You go swimming again."

They practiced the technique a few times, laughing and splashing, until she had the hang of it. The feeling of riding the board beneath the wave was exhilarating, like a day at a waterpark, but wilder and freer.

They were several hundred yards from shore now, and the waves were larger, well-spaced and regular. Drew straddled his board and motioned for her to do the same. "Are you ready to ride a wave?" he asked.

"Yes. I'm excited." Now that she was more comfortable in the water, she could hardly wait to experience the freedom she'd so often imagined.

"Okay, you want to watch for the wave and swing your board around to face the beach, then lie down and start paddling. Remember to keep your balance and don't lean back. Then remember that move I showed you on the beach."

"The push-up, jump-up thing," she said, thinking of other moves she wished he'd show her—moves that had nothing to do with surfing.

"Here comes a good wave," he said. "Let's go."

They turned their boards and started paddling. Sara tried to watch Drew out of the corner of her eye, to copy his moves, even as she struggled to balance and maneuver her own board.

Her first try was a disaster, as she immediately flipped off the board and sank like lead, the board tossing in the water behind her like a splinter from a shipwreck. She rose to the surface in time to see Drew ride his board into the shallows, as easily as if he'd been standing on the deck of a ship.

She managed to right her board and climb back on. He paddled back to her. "Don't worry, it'll get easier," he promised. "Ready to try again?"

She nodded. Everybody messed up their first time. She'd get it this time.

Round two wasn't much better. Round three she managed to get to her feet and promptly fell off the board.

"Maybe we should go in and rest," Drew said when he paddled to her after her fourth failed attempt.

"No." She threw herself back onto her board. "I'm going to do this."

"But if you're tired—"

"I'm fine." She glared at him.

He laughed. "Okay. We'll give it another try. Remember to keep your weight centered, and once you're on your feet, keep a low center of gravity."

She paddled out farther this time, hoping to buy more time to figure out the moves required to ride the wave. She watched the swells rolling in and turned toward shore once more, paddling hard as Drew had showed her.

She felt the moment the wave caught the board and began pulling it backward. Grabbing the sides of the board, she thrust herself up into a crouch, wobbling crazily as she slid her feet into position. Arms outstretched, she struggled to balance as the board pitched under her.

Then, in a magical moment, she found her balance. The board steadied and rose, carried on the wave. She was floating. Flying. Laughter bubbled in her like champagne and she turned her face up to the sun.

Even her less-than-graceful dismount in the shallows did nothing to dampen her enthusiasm. "I did it!" she shouted when Drew splashed toward her.

"You did it." His grin was as broad as hers felt, and he put his arm around her waist and hugged her to him as they waded to dry land.

"I want to do it again," she said.

"Let's rest a minute." He sat on the sand and unsnapped the leash from his ankle.

She dropped beside him and unleashed her board also, then lay on her back, one hand shielding her eyes from the bright sunlight. "I *am* tired," she said. "But thrilled."

Drew stretched out beside her, their bodies almost but not quite touching. "You did great," he said. "Now that you've got the balance thing figured out, you'll learn fast."

"Do you think I'll be able to compete in the tournament Saturday?"

"Sure. There's a new surfers division. You'll do fine in that."

"I can't wait." She rolled onto her stomach and propped herself on her elbows, looking down at him. "Thank you for teaching me. This is so much fun, being here with you like this."

"I'm enjoying it, too." His eyes met hers, the amusement she'd seen there earlier replaced by frank interest and desire. At least, she *thought* that's what the look said. She was out of practice at reading men. "So…no woman in your life?" She tried to sound casual, though her stomach was doing somersaults as she spoke. "Girlfriend? Significant other?"

He shook his head. "I've been so involved with Gus and the business, I haven't made time to date."

A sigh of relief escaped her. "I know what you mean."

"What about you?" he asked. "Any boyfriends back in L.A.?"

She shook her head. "No time." She'd told herself she'd date later, when the business was secure and she could afford to take more time off. But the business kept growing and there was always more to do. Then one day she'd looked up and she was twenty-six. More and more of her friends were married, living with someone or otherwise involved in serious relationships. Meanwhile she couldn't remember the last name of the last guy she'd dated.

"Sounds like we've both been working hard," Drew said, moving in closer. The look he gave her warmed her in a way the sun could not and burned away any shyness or hesitation that remained between them.

She leaned closer, her breast brushing his side, one hand braced on his arm. "I've been wanting all morning to kiss you," she whispered. "I don't want to wait anymore."

She lowered her lips to his and his arms came up to encircle her, pulling her down onto him. She angled her mouth more firmly against his and threaded her fingers through his hair. His lips were full and firm against hers, caressing sensitive nerve endings and sending waves of pleasure through her.

She opened her mouth, inviting his tongue, reveling in his taste of sweetness and salt. He smelled of seawater and clean sweat, and his skin beneath her hands was rough with sand.

He smoothed his hands down her back, caressing her skin, lingering over the indentation at the bottom of her spine, shaping his fingers to her buttocks and squeezing gently. A sharp ache of desire welled within her, making her catch her breath at its intensity. She could not remember when any man had affected her this way.

Hands on either side of her hips, he pulled her tight against him, letting her feel the fullness of his erection, pressing against her own throbbing sex until a soft moan escaped her. She felt drunk with desire, as free and energized as she had in those few moments of riding the wave.

She broke the kiss and smiled down at Drew. "I like your idea of resting," she said.

He reached up and brushed her hair back from her forehead. "I like you," he said. "And I want to see a lot more of you."

"I want to see a *lot* more of you." She emphasized the words with a bump-and-grind movement against him.

"Yeah." His voice was rough with desire. He smoothed his hands across her buttocks again. "I'd suggest we go back to my place right now, but Grandpa's liable to walk in any time."

"And Candy's working back at our beach house." Plus, Sara had never liked to bring guys to a place she shared with roommates. It was a personal rule of hers. Reluctantly, she pushed herself off him and sat in the sand.

He sat up and massaged her shoulder. "There's something to be said for anticipation." He lifted her hair to kiss the back of her neck, sending another wave of desire straight to her sex.

"Mmm." She closed her eyes and leaned against him. "Should we go back into the water?"

He glanced out at the ocean. "Waves are getting a little rough," he said.

For the first time, she noticed that the wind had picked up, ruffling her hair and blowing sand over them. The swells were larger now, breaking roughly into whitewater, tangles of seaweed bobbing among the foam. "Is a storm coming?" she asked.

He glanced at the sky, where the sun still shone. "Just a little afternoon turbulence."

She glanced at the sky also, and was surprised to find the sun considerably lower toward the horizon. "What time is it?" she asked.

He checked his watch. "It's after two. No wonder I'm starved." He rose and offered her his hand. "Come back to the shop with me. I need to see how things are going and we can grab some lunch."

"I really need to check in with my office," she said. Knowing Candy was slaving away made Sara feel guilty. She couldn't remember the last time she'd left Uncle Spence to his own devices so long. The thought made her stomach twist. He was probably having a panic attack.

They collected their boards and walked toward the more populated area of the shore. "I should probably try to get some work done this afternoon, too," Drew said, sounding reluctant.

"We could get together again tonight," she said. "And I should really be trying to get more points for the contest."

"We could check out the carnival," Drew said. "There are games and stuff there where I think you can win points."

"I'd love that." She squeezed his arm, enjoying the feel of the hard muscle of his bicep. "Ellie and Candy said something about a photo scavenger hunt on for tonight, too."

"A photo scavenger hunt?"

"You have to take pictures of certain things—I don't really know what, exactly. They're supposed to post a list tonight."

He laughed. "I'm game." He glanced at her. "As long as we can find some time to be alone, too."

She grinned. "I think that can definitely be arranged." Even if she had to hang a Do Not Disturb sign on her door in the beach house, she was determined to get Drew alone—and naked—before too many hours had passed.

4

SARA WAITED until she'd left Drew at the Surf Shack before she turned on her cell phone. She was disappointed, but not surprised, to see that her voice mail was full of messages, all from Uncle Spence. Each message was increasingly more irate, until by the last one he was reduced to almost hysterical sputtering.

With a sigh, Sara punched in his number as she made her way toward the beach house. "Uncle Spence, I just got your messages," she said. "What's up?"

"Sara! Where the hell have you been?" He rushed on, not waiting for an answer. "I can't find the Montoya file anywhere. And the survey company called, asking for the legal description of the McManus property. And where the hell is the ink for the fax machine?"

"The Montoya file is in the bottom right-hand drawer of my desk, under M. The legal description for the McManus property is available from the courthouse. Or you can look it up on the Web. The ink for the fax is in the supply cabinet. Top shelf." Honestly. How did the man function at home?

"Why aren't the files in the filing cabinet with everything else?" She could hear him slamming drawers and rummaging through papers.

"The files in the filing cabinet are completed transactions. The ones in my desk are current projects." She was sure she'd told him this before, but because he didn't expect to need the information, he hadn't bothered to remember it.

"I found them," he said. "When are you coming home? There's a lot of work here that needs your attention."

"Not until the end of the week. And it sounds as if you're handling everything fine." She shifted the phone to her other ear and forced optimism into her voice. "How did dinner with Mr. Granger go?"

"All right, I guess. He can be a real blowhard."

Then why do you hang out with him? But she knew the answer to that. Uncle Spence cultivated people who were good business contacts, not necessarily good friends. This lack of people he could really trust in his life probably accounted for why he depended so much on her. What he needed were other people in his life. Real friends. Maybe even a romantic interest.

"Whatever happened to that woman you were dating for a while?" she asked. "Martha?"

"Magda." A long silence. "She had to go back to Michigan to look after her father for a few months. After he died, we never got back together."

"You ought to give her a call. The two of you always had fun together."

"Maybe I should…" More rustling of papers. "I

don't have time for that now. Not while I'm trying to hold things together here with you gone."

"Everything will be fine," she said. "If anything else comes up, it can wait until I get back. It's only a few more days."

"People don't like to be kept waiting, Sara. I've always told you that."

"Waiting will teach them patience," she said, and laughed, picturing the shocked expression on Uncle Spence's face. Life was very serious business for him and she didn't usually try to persuade him otherwise.

"I need that information for the McManus property right away," he said. "Could you at least do that for me?"

The words to tell him to do it himself were there, on the tip of her tongue, but she couldn't bring herself to say them. Uncle Spence had always been very big on responsibility—as in her clients were her responsibility, even when she was on vacation. "All right. I'll look them up when I get back to the beach house and e-mail them to you. But anything else will have to wait until I get home."

"Keep your phone on in case I need you," he said. "I don't like being out of touch."

"Reception isn't always good out here," she lied. "I think the film crew's equipment must interfere with it or something."

"I don't know why those moviemakers have to take over public places when they've got acres of sound stages in Hollywood," he said.

She didn't bother to correct him. She was sure she'd told him about the *Sin on the Beach* festival, but of course, he hadn't bothered to pay attention to that, either.

Unlike Drew, who had focused on her every word. The memory of his attention made her feel warm all over, and her voice had a dreamy quality as she said goodbye to Spence and hung up. Thoughts of Drew accompanied her all the way back to the beach house.

Ellie was in the kitchen, slicing limes. "I'm starved," Sara said, heading for the refrigerator. "Where's Candy?"

"Out somewhere. I hope with Matt."

Sara fished a deli container of chicken salad out of the fridge, then plucked a fork from a drawer and dug in. "How was your day?" she asked. "How did the audition go?"

Ellie laid down the knife and turned to face Sara, her face serious. Sara's stomach tightened and she set aside her late lunch. "What happened? Did they give the part to someone else?"

"There was more than one part available." A smile lit Ellie's face and she bounced on her toes. "And I got one of them!"

"That's awesome!" Sara hugged her, then stepped back to look at her friend. Ellie wore the red bikini she'd borrowed from Sara, with a black fishnet cover-up. The new highlights in her hair and softer makeup had transformed her into a true beauty. "How could they not choose you? You're gorgeous."

Ellie executed a small curtsy, then turned back to the cutting board. "I'm making margaritas to celebrate. Want one?"

"Absolutely. I'm in the mood to celebrate."

"I take it your surfing lesson went well."

"It did. I actually surfed a wave. A small one, and only for a bit, but it was incredible." She took another bite of chicken salad. "Drew thinks I'll be in good shape for the beginner class of the competition."

"And how is Drew?" Ellie squeezed lime juice into the blender, then reached for a bottle of tequila.

"Drew is fine. Very fine indeed." She giggled. "I'm seeing him again tonight. He agreed to help us with the photo scavenger hunt." She leaned forward and nudged Ellie. "And how is Bill?"

A pink flush washed Ellie's cheeks as she added tequila to the blender. "He remembered me."

"And?"

"And…I think he liked what he saw." She slanted a look at Sara out of the corner of her eye. "I'm meeting him again in a little while."

"Then I'll make sure I'm out of the way." She finished the last of the salad and dropped the fork in the sink. "Drew and I want to check out the carnival."

"We'll meet you and Candy and Matt by the main festival stage at nine," Ellie said. "That's when the scavenger hunt starts." She added triple sec to the blender and dumped in ice.

Sara went into the living room, switching on the stereo as she passed. A bouncy rock tune filled the room and she danced her way over to her laptop. She hated even to turn the thing on, but she'd promised Uncle Spence. In any case, it wouldn't take a minute to search the county property records for the information he needed and e-mail it to him. Then she could change clothes and get ready for her date with Drew. She gave an extra hip shake at the thought of the evening ahead.

True to form, Uncle Spence called again while she was searching for the information. While she was talking him down, the door to the beach house opened and Candy sashayed in, followed by a good-looking guy who, on second-glance, proved to be Ellie's brother, Matt—sans glasses and his usual conservative threads, with a stylish new haircut and streaks in his hair.

Sara grinned and waved hello, then turned her attention back to business. "I'm sending the information right now, Uncle Spence," she said. "All you have to do is print it out."

When she got off the phone at last, she switched over to a spreadsheet she'd set up last night to track their points in the contest. She added in the points she'd earned today for entering the surfing competition, along with Ellie's points for landing the role in *Sin on the Beach.* "We're racking up the points," she said. "Take a look."

When everyone had oohed and ahhed over the totals for the Java Mamas—the name they'd chosen for their team, in honor of Ellie's coffee shop, where the three of them had met—and Ellie had given Sara a hard time about her businesslike approach to the contest, they debated ways to add to their total and made plans for the scavenger hunt later. Candy disappeared into Ellie's bedroom to change clothes and Sara followed her.

"Can I borrow something from you to wear tonight?" she asked.

"Sure." Candy stripped off her tank top and reached for the white bikini she'd laid out on the bed. "Anything you want."

"Something fun and flirty and…sexy." She folded her arms under her chest. "Nothing I own really qualifies." She'd packed mostly shorts and T-shirts, and one sundress, though it wasn't anything special.

"Hoping to impress a certain hunky surfer?" Candy asked. She reached back to fasten the swimsuit top.

Sara grinned. "I'm hoping to speed up his heart rate a little."

"I've got just the thing." She stepped into the bikini bottoms. "My suitcase is in the front closet. Inside there's a red rayon halter dress—cut down to there and up to here." She indicated a spot somewhere around her navel. "You'll be a red-hot mama in it, I promise."

Sara laughed. "Thanks." She glanced toward the living room, where she could just make out Ellie and Matt's voices above the music from the stereo. "So how are things going with you and Matt?"

"I think I'm impressing him with my work ethic." She turned to the mirror and fluffed her hair.

"Girl, in that suit, I don't think your work ethic is

the first thing that will come to mind," Sara said. The white suit set off Candy's golden tan and accented every curve.

She sighed. "Can't blame a girl for trying, but he wants to get back with his old girlfriend."

"Then he's crazy."

Candy shrugged. "It's all right. It's probably a bad idea to get involved with my boss, anyway. Right now, we're having fun. If I can get that team leader position I want, I'll be happy."

"Take it from one who knows—building your life around work can be a big mistake."

Candy patted her arm. "I know. It's all about balance. We're both working on that this week, right?" She turned from the mirror. "Do I look ready to limbo?"

"You're going to limbo?"

"Sure. Thirty points for entering. Two hundred and fifty if I win."

Sara laughed. "You look ready for anything."

"I'll show them how low I can go." Candy laughed.

Sara nodded. "Thanks for lending me the dress."

"No problem. See you later. And good luck."

She didn't think she'd need much luck with Drew. It was obvious he was attracted to her, and whenever they were together she could practically feel the electricity. More than luck, she needed courage—the courage to set practicality and logic aside and take more risks. The courage to ride the wave of emotion they were on, and not worry about the possible rough landing later.

WHEN THE SUN went down, the beach took on a
Mardi Gras atmosphere. Music blared from giant
speakers set up on the sand, tiki torches flared and
bright neon glowed from the carnival rides and
midway. The laid-back surfers and playing children
of earlier in the day were replaced by groups of
young adults, their laughter and revelry drowning out
the sound of the crashing waves. The scents of french
fry grease, beer and sugary cotton candy filled the
air.

Sara met Drew at the pier. His eyes glowed with appreciation when he saw her. "I like this dress," he said,
staring down at the swell of cleavage displayed by the
plunging neckline of the fire-engine-red halter dress.

"I borrowed it from Candy." Nothing in her
current wardrobe was so daring, but she was thinking
when she returned home, that might change. It
wouldn't hurt to bring out her inner wild child a little
more in her everyday life.

They headed toward the music and lights. As they
approached the entrance to the carnival they heard
the throbbing beat of "Limbo Rock" and the raucous
cheers of a crowd.

"It's the limbo contest," Sara said. She stood on
tiptoe, trying to see over the throng to the cleared
area where the contest was being held.

"How *low* can you go?" boomed an announcer,
and more cheers erupted from the spectators.

"I can't see a thing," Sara said. "And we'll never
get through that mob."

"Maybe I can help." He bent and she let out a yelp

as he hoisted her onto his shoulders. She wrapped her legs around his head and clutched at his hair, aware of the muscles of his shoulders knotting beneath her thighs and his hands holding firmly to her waist— not to mention the back of his head against her crotch. "Can you see?" he asked.

She'd forgotten all about the limbo contest, but directed her attention to the line of dancing men and women taking turns shimmying under a bamboo pole. "I see Candy!" she said, raising her voice to be heard above the driving beat of the music. She watched in awe as her friend appeared to be almost levitating her body off the sand, sliding under the pole with a suppleness Sara was sure she herself had never possessed. "She's amazing."

"I think you're pretty amazing." His hands had slid lower, to grasp her hips. He peered up at her from the silky folds of the dress. "This is an interesting view."

She laughed, feeling a little self-conscious, and also wanting to be closer to him. "Put me down," she said. "This should be a perfect time to check out the carnival, while everyone's watching the limbo."

"Don't you want to stick around and see if your friend wins?"

She shook her head. "Nobody's going to beat Candy. She's a real competitor, even when it comes to partying."

Drew lowered her to the ground, sliding her body in front of his, the skirt of the dress riding up as she slid. He helped her smooth it down, his eyes never leaving her face. "I've been thinking about that kiss this afternoon," he said.

She stopped fussing with the dress and looked into his eyes. "I've been thinking about it, too."

"I'm thinking we should try again. See if it was as wonderful as I remember."

"Good idea." She felt lightheaded at the thought.

And then his mouth was on hers, and she was sure she had been waiting all day to feel him this way again. Though only their mouths touched, she felt the connection in every part of he body.

She was tempted to forget about the carnival and everything else and drag him back to the beach house right this minute. But she'd promised to help with the scavenger hunt. She hated to let her friends down—even for Drew. Reluctantly she pulled away and smiled up at him. "Are you hungry?" she asked.

"Yes." The way his eyes swept over her, she had a feeling he had an appetite for more than food.

"I'm starved," she said. "Let's eat something fattening, greasy and absolutely amazing."

Hand in hand, they walked to the carnival midway, and followed the scent of hot grease and sugar to the food booths, where they purchased a junk-food feast of corny dogs, onion rings and funnel cakes, with sodas to wash everything down. "My taste buds are in heaven," she moaned as she licked mustard from the side of her corn dog.

"You're making parts of me pretty happy, watching you eat that," he said. "Want some more mustard?"

She laughed. "You ought to see what I can do with a Bomb Pop."

He groaned. "Maybe you can show me later."

They strolled past the Ferris wheel, Tilt-a-Whirl and scorpion. "Want to take a spin?" Drew asked.

She ate the last onion ring then wiped her hands. "Think I'd better pass. I've avoided all of those whirly rides since I was sixteen and ate two chili dogs, then rode the teacups at the county fair." She made a face. "The results were not pretty."

He laughed. "Okay, no rides. What, then?"

They had reached the section of the carnival devoted to games of skill and chance. A large sign declared that winners of each game could receive points toward *Sin on the Beach* Festival prizes. "Let's play some games," she said, approaching a booth.

"Step right up," said the teenage boy behind the counter, doing his best to deepen his voice. "Knock over three targets and win a prize."

"Looks easy enough." Drew handed over a dollar and accepted three baseballs.

She stepped back as he wound up. His first pitch flattened a target on the top of three rows of plastic bullseyes. Sara clapped and cheered. "Way to go, Drew!"

He fired a second ball and it took out a target in the middle row.

"Only one more and you win a prize," the carny intoned less than enthusiastically.

Looking determined, Drew reared back and fired. The ball made a loud *thunk!* as it landed on the support just below the bottom row of targets.

"Too bad," the carny said. "Want to try again?"

Drew shook his head and he and Sara walked away. "I knew I should have tried out for the baseball team instead of spending all that time surfing."

She laughed and took his arm. "Let's try something else." She spotted a target-shooting booth. "That one. My turn this time."

She paid the woman behind the counter and took her position behind one of the mounted guns. A row of yellow plastic ducks on a moving conveyor at the other end of the booth were her target. "Hit a duck, you get the number of points displayed on the duck," the woman explained. "You get six shots."

Sara bent low and closed one eye, sighting down the barrel of the rifle to the ducks, which were marked ten, twenty or thirty points, with the occasional fifty or hundred pointer at irregular intervals. She took aim and squeezed the trigger.

With a metallic *ping!* the duck fell. "Hey, you got him," Drew said.

She smiled and fixed on another thirty-point duck. This one fell also.

In the end, she hit five ducks and earned a hundred and thirty points. "You didn't tell me you were a sharp-shooter," Drew said, grinning at her.

"When I was in high school my girlfriend and I used to skip school and spend the afternoon out at Pacific Park," she said. "She was dating a guy who worked there and he'd get us in free."

"Skipping school to hang out at the midway. You were a wild child."

"I had a hard time fitting in after we moved here from Georgia," she said. "And I missed my dad." She glanced at him. "I guess you could say it took me awhile to get my head on straight." Skipping school wasn't the worst of what she'd done back then. Some of the places she'd hung out had been popular with gangs and drug dealers. She'd been too naive to know how much danger she'd been in, or too rebellious to care. Only in retrospect could she see how lucky she'd been to survive those turbulent years with few scars.

Drew put his arm around her. "We all make mistakes when we're young and foolish," he said. "But it looks like you've turned out all right. More than all right."

She smiled up at him. With him, she felt she could do no wrong. Was it the man or the location? This beach festival was all about music and lights, glamour and sex. Everything was exotic and exciting—so different from the practical world she usually inhabited. She felt like a different person here—one who was more willing to take chances.

The sound of clinking glasses and raucous laughter drifted from an open-air bar, where strings of colored lights lent a festive air to the crowds of celebrating revelers. "This reminds me of New Orleans and Mardi Gras," Sara said. "Or at least, what I imagine it's like. I've never actually been."

"No beads and no one asking you to show them your tits," Drew said.

She laughed. "The night is young."

They were near the entrance to the carnival once more, and a brightly lit stage with a banner announcing Magellan the All-Knowing. A crowd was beginning to gather as a man in a green turban and Hawaiian shirt, microphone in hand, called out, "Come one, come all. Prepare to play Truth or Bare."

"Truth or *bare?*" Sara laughed.

"You laugh!" The entertainer's words startled her, and she tried to hide behind Drew, but the man had spotted her. "You can't hide from the all knowing one." His voice boomed from the speakers. "You shall be my first contestant. You and your young man there."

Drew glanced at her. "Do you want to leave?"

"What time is it? I don't want to be late for the scavenger hunt."

He checked his watch. "It's 7:35."

"Then let's play. I want to win more points." She pointed to a sign beside the stage that promised Magellan's guests could receive points.

Drew followed her up a short flight of steps to the stage. "What's your name?" Magellan asked.

"If you're all-knowing you shouldn't have to ask," Drew said.

The crowd laughed and Magellan scowled. "Andrew, perhaps you'd like to tell the crowd your girlfriend's name."

Sara gasped and turned to look at Drew, who was staring at the turbaned entertainer. "Nobody calls me Andrew," he said.

Magellan grinned. "It's the name on your birth certificate, isn't it?"

"How did you—"

"Magellan the All-Knowing knows these things." He smirked at the crowd, who applauded and cheered. Then he stuck the microphone in front of Sara. "Tell us your name, dear."

"Sara." She stared out at the sea of faces at her feet and began to feel nervous. What had she been thinking, coming up here?

"Are you ready to play Truth or Bare?" Magellan asked.

She took a deep breath and regained some of her composure. "How do you play?" she asked.

"It's very simple. I'm going to tell you something about yourself that's true. If I'm wrong, you get fifty points and free tickets for the carnival rides."

"What if you're right?" Drew asked.

Magellan grinned. "It's called Truth or *Bare*. You figure it out."

The crowd hooted with laughter. Sara glanced at Drew. Considering she was wearing only the dress and a pair of panties, she could be in trouble. Drew at least had a shirt he could remove before his shorts and whatever he was wearing underneath.

Or maybe he was wearing nothing underneath. The thought made her a little breathless.

"I'll go first," Drew said. Sara wondered if he was being chivalrous, or if he was skeptical of the carnival prophet. Magellan studied him a long moment, his dark eyebrows pulled together in a V. He put one hand to his forehead and closed his eyes and after a moment said, in a loud, dramatic voice,

"Your truth is that there is an emptiness in your life you've tried to fill with work and family—but it isn't enough."

Drew looked startled, his face pale in the bright stage lights. Magellan lowered his hand and opened his eyes. "Truth, or bare?" he asked.

Drew hesitated a second, then pulled his shirt over his head. Someone in the crowd let out a loud wolf whistle and everyone laughed.

Sara took his hand in hers and squeezed it. Magellan's prophecy, and the fact that Drew had admitted it was true, surprised her. He seemed like such a together guy. What was the emptiness in his life?

Magellan turned to Sara. The crowd roared with approval. The soothsayer gave an exaggerated leer. "That's not much of a dress there, is it?" he said.

She shook her head and swallowed hard. "No."

He took both her hands in his, forcing her to let go of Drew. "There's nothing to be afraid of," he crooned.

She felt a warmth surge through her. Not a sexual heat—more as if she'd been plunged into a hot bath. Magellan closed his eyes and ruminated while the crowd remained hushed, almost reverent.

Sara glanced at Drew. He was frowning. What would he think if she dropped her dress in front of all these people? Would he enjoy the view, or turn away in embarrassment?

He took a step back, and she tried to turn her head to follow him with her eyes, but Magellan commanded her attention. "Look at me," he said.

She looked into his eyes, black and penetrating, and suppressed a shiver. Then he smiled, a slow lifting of his lips and a flashing of white teeth. "I have discovered your truth," he announced.

The crowd applauded and hooted. Sara resisted the urge to fold her arms over her breasts. All the daring she'd felt earlier had deserted her.

"You're trying to pay a debt you do not owe," Magellan addressed her sternly. "You think by denying yourself what you really want you'll make up for past mistakes. But those mistakes are long forgotten by everyone but you."

She stared at him, unsure she had really heard him. Had he spoken, or was that only her own subconscious taunting her?

"Truth...or bare?"

"Bare! Bare! Bare!" the crowd shouted.

She looked around for Drew, but he was nowhere to be found. Panic fluttered in her heart. Where had he gone? Had he deserted her rather than be part of her scandalous behavior?

"What is your answer?" Magellan prompted.

She looked back at him, and opened her mouth to lie, but the words weren't in her. If he knew that much, he would know she wasn't telling the truth. She *was* trying to repay a debt to Uncle Spence, though she couldn't accept that she didn't owe him. He had literally saved her life when she'd been racing toward disaster. How could she not give him something in return?

She nodded her head.

"Is that a yes?" Magellan asked, his expression gleeful.

"Yes," she whispered, then in a stronger voice, "Yes." She took a deep breath and looked out over the crowd. What did it matter if she dropped the dress? She didn't know any of these people. And she'd told herself she wanted to be more daring.

Maybe not quite this daring, but what choice did she have now? She'd given her word, as it were, and she had never before gone back on her word.

She reached up and fumbled with the tie at the neck of the dress. From somewhere the familiar *ba-da-da, da-da-da-da!* of stripper music blared.

The knot was stubborn, and her fingers were slick with nervous sweat. But finally it was undone. She forced herself to lift her head, to stare out, not at the crowd, but over their heads, imagining only Drew was looking at her—that she was doing this for him.

But where had he gone? Why had he abandoned her now?

"Come on dear, everyone is waiting," Magellan said.

She nodded, and dropped the ends of the ties. The fabric slid down over her breasts, cool and slippery, and she felt the night breeze pucker her nipples.

Scarcely was she uncovered, though, before the stage and all around them were plunged into darkness.

5

DREW FOUND Sara on the darkened stage and took her arm. "Back here," he whispered. "Come this way." He led her down steps at the back of the stage, then through a narrow alley between the stage and the Tilt-a-Whirl. Only when they were some distance away did he stop and turn to her. "You'd better, um…" He motioned to her dress.

Though she'd managed to cover one breast with one of the strips of fabric, she'd lost her hold on the other and her left breast was bare. Blushing, she fumbled with the fabric.

"Here, let me." Gently, he turned her around and tied the ends of the halter once more, then moved his hands to her shoulders, where they rested, heavy and warm.

She leaned against him, as stirred by his gentleness as by the knowledge that, for a moment at least, she had been practically naked in front of him.

He kissed the top of her head, then the back of her neck, his lips hot against her skin. His hands slid down her arms to her waist, then up to cup her breasts. She held her breath, wanting more but unsure if now was the time—or the place—to ask for it.

He moved his hands up, then brushed lightly across her breasts. She sucked in a sharp breath and felt her nipples pucker and harden. "Yes," she whispered, so softly she wasn't sure he'd heard her.

In any case, he understood what she wanted. He began to stroke her nipples, first with his palms, then with two fingers, plucking and fondling the distended nubs until she felt her knees weaken, and braced herself against him to keep from falling. His hands stilled. "Do you want me to stop?"

She shook her head. "No!"

"Good. Because I don't want to stop." He trailed kisses along her shoulder, all the while his fingers caressed her. The sensation of silky fabric sliding across sensitized flesh was almost too much to bear. She gasped and writhed against him, feeling the hard ridge of his erection against her backside.

He moved to her sides and slipped his hands beneath the fabric of the dress. She sighed as his hands covered her naked breasts. She felt hot all over, his hands hotter still as he continued to fondle and tease her.

"I think maybe I tied this too soon," he said.

"Yes." She reached up and helped him unfasten the knot, then turned to face him. He hadn't replaced his shirt and the feel of his warm skin against her breasts was exquisite. She stroked her hands across the fine mat of hair on his chest and sighed.

"What happened?" she asked.

"I slipped behind the stage and disconnected the lights," he said.

She laughed. "You didn't!"

She felt him smile, his lips curving against the top of her head, where he pressed against her. "I did."

"Thank you." She kissed his pec. "I'm really not an exhibitionist, you know."

"I figured as much. But you could say I did it because I'm selfish."

"Selfish?" She looked up, wishing she could see more of his face in the darkness.

"I wanted to be the only one to see you naked tonight."

They kissed, an intense coupling of lips and tongues, pressed as close to one another as they could get with the barrier of clothing. He slipped his hand beneath the skirt of her dress and squeezed her bottom, while she wrapped one leg around his hip and encircled him with her arms.

A burst of laughter from somewhere nearby stilled them both. Sara looked around, aware that though they were hidden in the shadows, the midway and hundreds, maybe thousands of people were only a few steps away. "We can't stay here," she said.

Drew nodded. "Can we go back to your place?"

She shook her head. "Ellie or Candy might come in and, well, I'd really like to go somewhere we could be truly alone."

"Grandpa is at my place. Tonight is his poker night."

She groaned and rested her head against him. "I'm about ready to pull you down right here in the sand."

"I know a place." He took her hand in his. "Come on."

She pulled from his grasp and hastily tied the ends of the halter again. "Where?"

"It's nearby. And no one will interrupt us there, but hurry."

The last command was completely unnecessary. She had never been in more of a hurry in her life. If she and Drew didn't make love, and soon, she was afraid she might explode from sheer frustration. She much preferred to experience fireworks of a very different kind.

DREW HADN'T been to the old lifeguard shack since last season, but it was just as it had been for years. The weathered wooden building sat on the beach at one end of the pier, a large padlock affixed to the door, next to a sign that declared Authorized Personnel Only!

"Are you authorized personnel?" Sara asked.

"Sort of. I worked two years as a lifeguard when I was in high school and college." He led her to the window around back and felt along the lower edge. "There's a trick to opening this." He leaned his weight on the frame and felt the metal give enough for him to pop his finger beneath it. A sharp tug and the window slid open. He turned to Sara and made a step with his hand. "You first, m'lady."

She laughed and stepped into his hand and let him boost her through the window. He had a tantalizing view of her firm, round bottom as she hoisted herself over the sill. Then he pulled himself up after her.

There was just enough illumination from the lights of the pier to make out an old sofa and a card table and chairs. An empty cooler sat in the corner, and various bulletins and old schedules were tacked to the walls. "What is this place?" she asked, looking around.

"It's where the lifeguards take their breaks or have lunch and stuff." He pounded the sofa cushions, hoping no mice would run out. Nothing like vermin to spoil the mood. But not even much dust rose from the upholstery.

She moved into his arms. "So we're really not supposed to be here."

"Not technically. But it will be all right. No one ever comes here."

"How did you know about the window?"

He grinned. "I guess the lifeguards still come here to make out. But if they hear us they'll just go away. It's an unwritten rule. You don't mind, do you?"

She smoothed her hands down his arms. "I think it's kind of exciting." It reminded her of the thrill skipping school and getting away with shoplifting had given her when she was a teen. But there was nothing illegal or dangerous about being here with Drew.

He pulled her tight against him, letting her feel how turned on he was. "Speaking of excited…"

She silenced him with a kiss, plunging her tongue between his lips and pressing her thigh between his legs, stroking him through his shorts. He bunched the skirt of her dress in his hands, the silky fabric sliding through his fingers as he nuzzled her neck. She smelled like oranges and vanilla, both exotic and familiar.

She reached back and untied the halter top of her dress, freeing her breasts once more. He gathered her in both hands, and felt her jerk beneath him as he stroked her nipples. When he bent and sucked the tip of one breast into his mouth, she moaned, and he pulled her closer, wanting to touch every part of her.

He moved his mouth to her other breast, and slipped his hands beneath her skirt. The skin at the top of her buttocks was like silk beneath his fingers as he hooked his thumbs beneath the elastic of her panties. He couldn't wait any longer to feel her naked. He shoved the underwear down and squeezed her buttocks, pressing his fingers into her firm flesh, forcing her tighter still against his straining cock. "You feel so good," he groaned into her ear.

She responded by reaching down and unfastening the tie at the waist of his board shorts, and slipping her hand in to stroke his penis. He shuddered at her touch, and pushed her gently onto the sofa, then stripped out of his shorts and tossed them aside.

He was naked now, and she was nearly so, covered only by the bunched fabric of the dress around her waist. The pinkish vapor light from the docks bathed her in a rosy glow. She smiled up at him. "I like what I see." Her gaze shifted to his cock. "Very much."

He knelt beside her on the couch and helped her out of the dress. He was about to toss it on the floor with his clothes when she stopped him. "It's not my dress." Then she draped it carefully over one of the chairs and lay back again. "Where were we?"

He covered her with his body and kissed her, the head of his penis nudging at her entrance. She was hot and wet and it was all he could do not to plunge himself into her immediately.

As if reading his thoughts—or maybe it was that her thoughts were along the same line—she broke off the kiss and looked up at him. "We need a condom," she said.

He stared at her, blinking, and feeling a little desperate. "I don't have one." He'd stopped carrying condoms in his wallet shortly after high school.

She smiled. "That's okay. I do. In my bag."

He didn't wait for an explanation, but levered himself up off the sofa and found her purse where she'd dropped it by the window. "Look in the center zipper pocket," she said.

He found the condom packet, then noticed the soft glow of the light from her cell phone. "All right if I switch off your phone?" he asked.

She laughed. "Good idea."

He found the right button and listened to the phone shut down. No sense risking an interruption.

Back on the sofa, she reached for the condom packet, but he set it aside. "Not yet," he said.

Some of his earlier urgency had subsided, leaving him wanting to savor this time with her more—to make it as good as it could be.

He slid to his knees on the floor and swung her around to face him. "What are you—?"

She fell silent when he draped her legs across his shoulders and put his mouth on her clit. The hard bud of her arousal jumped beneath his tongue and he pressed firmly against it. "Ohhh," she said, a sound of pure pleasure and need.

Hands on her inner thighs, he parted her legs farther, feeling the tension in her muscles, the urgency within her building with each stroke of his tongue. She writhed beneath him, responsive to his every movement. His cock twitched in sympathy, and he ached to bury himself in her.

But not yet.

He slid his hands beneath her bottom, drawing her closer still. She grasped his head in her hands, her fingers entwined in his hair, caressing him. The tenderness of the gesture moved him, intensifying his desire, leaving him literally trembling.

He drew her clit into his mouth, sucking hard, and she cried out and bucked beneath him. She gasped and rocked against him, saying his name over and over, "Drew, Drew, Drewdrewdrewdrewdrew."

He laughed and rose to kneel over her again. He fumbled with the condom packet. "Here, let me," she said, and tore it open and reached out to roll it on.

He watched her, transfixed by the sight of her hands moving over his penis, as aroused by the image as by the feel of her stroking across those most sensitive of nerve endings. When she was done, she smiled up at him, then spread her legs wider and guided him into her.

He closed his eyes and groaned at the sensation of heat and pressure, then rocked forward, unable to hold back any longer. She grasped his buttocks, encouraging him, rising up to meet each thrust with one of her own. He braced his arms on either side of her, grasping the back of the couch, thrusting hard now, each parry and retreat building toward release.

He came with a shout—of triumph and joy and half a dozen other emotions he couldn't name. When he could open his eyes he looked down at Sara, and she was smiling. He smiled in return, then they laughed and embraced. "That was pretty amazing," he murmured as they shifted around to lie next to each other.

"Pretty amazing," she echoed, settling her head in the hollow of his shoulder.

He smoothed his hand over her hair, thoughts whirling in his head like a crazy carnival ride. He'd known Sara not even two days, yet sex with her had been more intense than any he'd known before. Was it simply a matter of physical compatibility, or was something else at work here?

When he'd stood on that stage and removed his shirt, he'd publicly acknowledged something he'd tried not to think about for a long time now. He didn't know how Magellan had learned his secret, but the colorful carny had hit it on the nose: something, or someone, was missing in his life. Sara might be the one who could fill that empty space—at least for the rest of the week she was here.

FORGET DRUGS or alcohol—Sara now knew true euphoria. Not to mention elation, sexual fulfillment and a few other emotions she couldn't name. Drew gave new meaning to *good in bed*. Or maybe it was only that she was so ready for someone like him in her life they couldn't have failed to click.

"What did that Magellan dude mean when he said you were trying to pay a debt you didn't owe?" Drew asked.

"I think he was talking about my Uncle Spence. At least that was my interpretation." She shifted, making herself more comfortable on the narrow couch. "Even though he can be a pain sometimes, I feel I owe him so much. I was pretty much a juvenile delinquent when he came into my life. I'd have probably ended up in jail or dead if he hadn't straightened me out."

"Are those the mistakes Magellan talked about— the ones everyone's forgotten but you?"

"It doesn't matter if no one else remembers them. I know how close I came to ruining my life."

"But you've done a lot for your uncle since then, right?" he said. "Working for him and all?"

"Yes." But could she ever do enough for the man who had literally saved her life? "Working for him is the only job I've really ever had. He's given me a lot of responsibility in the company and I don't want to let him down."

"Sounds like he's putting a lot of pressure on you."

She sighed. "It feels that way sometimes. Though I do like my job. Most of the time."

"My Grandpa Gus is just the opposite," Drew said. "He still thinks he can do everything he did when he was my age—run the Surf Shack, catch waves *and* be a local character. Now he's got this part in this TV show."

"Maybe all those things help keep him young."

"Worrying about him is making *me* old. I mean, the man's had two heart attacks. He needs to slow down."

"He's lucky to have you to worry about him and try to lighten his load," she said. "Just like Uncle Spence is lucky to have me."

"I know I haven't done much the past couple of days, spending time on the beach with you." His arm tightened around her. "Because you're only here for a week, I want to see you as much as I can. But since I came here two years ago, I've been putting in some long hours. Grandpa had kind of let things slide and it took me awhile to straighten out all the books and inventory records and bring them up to date. Between that and looking after him I haven't had a lot of time for myself."

The thing was, he knew he had a good life. He lived in a great place and surfed almost as much as he wanted. To most people it looked like a perpetual vacation. The fact that that wasn't enough for him made him feel guilty sometimes.

"Speaking of time." She raised her head to look around the shack. "What time is it?"

He squinted at his watch. "It's a little before nine."

She sat up and climbed over him and began searching for her clothes in the dark. "I almost forgot about the scavenger hunt. You don't mind do you? I promised my friends, and I haven't contributed very many points to the contest."

"It's fine. It'll be fun." He handed her her panties and pulled her close to kiss her. "I'd have fun doing anything with you."

THE LIGHTS were back on as they raced past the entrance to the carnival and Magellan, who was working his magic on another hapless couple. They made it to the main stage and found Ellie, who introduced them to Bill, a dark-skinned man with a soul patch, a gold earring and a cat-like sensuality.

Candy and Matt joined them, proudly displaying her limbo trophy. "I saw you," Ellie said. "You were terrific. I don't see how you bend that way."

"Years of gymnastics and ballet," she said.

"I can't even do half the positions in my yoga class," Sara said.

"Shhh," Ellie said. "They're starting."

A perky young woman in a silver bikini went over the rules for the competition: a list of the photos required would be shown on the screen behind her in a moment. All entry photos had to be submitted to the contest cell number before midnight. The winner would be selected on the basis of quality, creativity, completeness and timeliness. "Is everybody ready?" she asked.

"Yes!" the crowd responded, with accompanying whoops and hollers.

"Then here we go." The list of items they were to photograph flashed on the large screen behind the stage and chaos erupted as each team scrambled to organize itself.

Ellie took charge. "Okay, quick," she addressed them. "Innie or outie?"

"Drew has an innie," Sara volunteered, caught up in the excitement of the hunt.

"And Sara has an outie." He grinned at her.

"Quick, shirts up. Let's see them," Ellie said, readying her camera phone.

"I'm not wearing a shirt," Sara protested.

"It won't hurt anyone to see your underwear," Ellie argued. "Now hurry."

Laughing, Sara stood beside Drew and on cue they flashed their navels at the camera. Then he grabbed her hand and they took off in search of the items on their list.

"Where are we going to find a woman sucking on an ice pop and a woman in a thong who'll let us take a picture of her backside?" Drew asked.

"Not to mention a tattoo of a naked woman and a woman in a wet T-shirt?" Sara said. She stopped and dug in her purse. "First, I'd better turn on my phone." As soon as she did, the message tone sounded. She ignored it. "It will be Uncle Spence," she said. "I refuse to talk to him now."

"What does he want at this time of night?" Drew asked.

"Maybe just to talk. He lives by himself and sometimes he calls just because he's lonely—though he'd never admit it." She ignored the guilt that pinched at her at the thought. "I've been trying to get him to start dating again or join a club or something, but he has a hard time doing new things."

"I know where we can find the tattoo." Drew said.

"Where's that?"

"Big Richard over at Tiny's Tattoos has one on his chest." He grinned. "A naked woman on a surfboard."

She laughed and they set off for the tattoo parlor, which was located one block from the pier. When they arrived, a beefy, bare-chested man was posing for a group of onlookers. "You here for a picture, too?" asked the woman behind the front counter.

"Yeah." Drew held up Sara's camera phone. "It's for a contest."

The woman nodded. "Go right ahead. Big Richard likes showing off."

When it was their turn, Richard obligingly posed. While Drew snapped the photo, Sara admired the busty blonde depicted riding the waves on the left side of his chest. "It's my wife," Richard explained. "I had it done for our anniversary."

"How sweet," she said. In a way.

One picture down, they left the shop in a hurry, squeezing past other photographers in the doorway. "Looks like a lot of people know about Big Richard," Sara said.

"Yeah. Just don't ever make the mistake of calling him Dick."

She laughed. "Right. What's next?"

Drew checked the list. "A woman sucking an ice pop, a woman in a wet T-shirt or a woman in a thong."

"The carnival sells ice pops," she said. "And keep your eye out for a woman in a thong."

"Too bad you're not wearing a thong," Drew mused.

They cut across the midway on their way to the ice pop stand and almost collided with two men and a woman huddled beneath a floodlight. "Watch where you're going!" one of the men barked, scowling at them.

He was holding a camera phone and Sara saw now that the woman was bent over the second man's bare buttock, a marker in her hand. As soon as she and Drew were past the group, Sara pulled Drew close and whispered. "I think she was *drawing* a birthmark on that guy's butt."

"What? Why would she do that?"

"It's one of the items on the scavenger hunt list. I remember seeing it."

He shrugged. "I guess that's one way to handle it."

"Drew! That's cheating."

He laughed. "It's just a silly contest."

She shook her head. "I don't like it. Cheating takes all the fun out of something like this."

He put his arm around her and pulled her close. "I love that you're so honest. I promise you we won't cheat. And we'll win anyway."

They made it to the ice pop stand. "This one's easy. I'll photograph you with the ice pop."

"Okay." She grinned at him. Her phone buzzed and she glanced at the screen, relief flooding her when she saw the call wasn't from Spence. "It's Candy with some of her photos." She laughed and turned the screen toward Drew, showing a trio of naked male rear ends, followed by three women flashing their breasts at the camera. "These are hilarious," she said.

Drew admired Candy's photos, then handed Sara an ice pop. "Here you go."

She unwrapped the treat, feeling a little self-conscious. But hey, this festival was no place for that. She put on her best come-hither look and slid the pop into her mouth, then made a show of working her tongue around it.

"Oh man," Drew breathed, and took the shot. "I could stand here all night watching you eat that thing—though as hot as you look, it'll probably melt away in another few seconds."

She laughed and dumped the pop in a nearby trash can. "We still have a lot of pictures to take."

He checked the list on the phone. "A woman in a thong and a woman in a wet T-shirt," he said. He looked around. "I'm not seeing either."

"I could borrow your shirt and we could stage the wet T-shirt photo," Sara said. "That is, if you wouldn't mind getting it wet."

He grinned. "You can do anything you want with it." He looked around. "Where should we take the picture?"

"Let's find someplace on the beach that's not too

busy," she said. "I don't want to strip down in front of just anyone."

"Right." He took her arm and they headed away from the carnival, toward the section of beach where they'd surfed that morning.

The noise and lights of the festival faded as they moved along the shore, replaced by the glow of moonlight on sand and the hypnotic rhythm of the waves. Sara kicked off her sandals and stuffed them in her bag and Drew carried his in one hand, his other arm around her. "This is so beautiful," she said, resting her head on his shoulder. "So peaceful."

"It is." He stopped and turned toward her. "Is this private enough for your photo shoot?"

She nodded. The lights of the festival were a glow in the distance and no one was on this deserted stretch of beach. "Give me your shirt. I'll put it on, then let you take care of Candy's dress while I wade into the ocean. Then you can take a picture. Don't forget the flash."

He dropped his sandals and pulled off his shirt and handed it to her. She slipped the shirt over her head, pausing to breathe deeply of his scent that clung to it. The fabric was warm from his skin, and she instantly recalled their lovemaking in the lifeguard shack, and how wonderful she'd felt in his arms.

Smiling at him, she untied the dress and slid it down her hips and handed it to him. He laughed. "You could wear my shirt as a dress if you wanted."

She glanced down. The shirt came to mid-thigh on her. "Not exactly stylish," she said.

"Looks great to me." He tossed the dress over his shoulder and readied the camera phone. "Time to get wet."

She turned toward the ocean. The tide was low and the surface was calm, gentle waves lapping at the shore. She waded out until water covered the hem of the shirt, then ducked down, wetting herself to her neck. She was surprised at how warm the water was, but when she rose the breeze chilled her, stiffening her nipples so they poked at the fabric of the shirt. "How's this?" she asked, standing.

"Beautiful." He took a few steps toward her and the camera flashed.

"You didn't get my face, did you?" she asked. "Take another one." She covered her face with her hands, a see-no-evil pose.

He laughed and the camera flashed again. "You look great."

She started to walk out of the water, but he stopped her. "Wait. I'm coming in with you." He ran back up the sand and left Candy's dress and her phone with her purse and their shoes, then splashed out to meet her.

"You goof. Now we're both soaked," she said.

He pulled her into his arms. "So? I spend all my spare time in this ocean. I felt like spending a little more of it with you now." He kissed her, a lingering caress.

She slipped her arms around his neck and opened her mouth for his tongue, rocked against him by the current. All sense of time escaped her as they learned every nuance of each other's mouths, testing the sensitivity of a bottom lip, or the angle of a corner, or the response to a gentle nip.

Lips still locked to hers, he grasped her thighs and twined her legs around his waist, then began walking out, into deeper water. "What are you doing?" she asked.

"I want to make love to you," he said. "Right here. Right now."

6

"YES," she said. It was what she wanted too. Here in this world of sky and water, with only the murmur of the waves and the wind in their ears, they might have been the only two people on earth. Schedules and obligations seemed a distant memory. Nothing mattered but here and now, and the need of her body for his.

Keeping her legs wrapped around him and supporting her with one hand, he slipped his other hand between them and pulled aside the crotch of her panties, exposing her sex to the warm sea water and to his exploring fingers. Parting her lips, he plunged two fingers into her. She leaned back her head and groaned, tightening her muscles around him.

"You're so wet," he murmured in her ear, and nibbled her earlobe.

The gesture sent a shiver down her spine, and she locked her legs more firmly around him. He removed his fingers from her and fumbled at the waistband of his shorts.

"If you lose those, you'll have to walk home naked," she said.

"Then I'd better be careful." He shoved the shorts to his knees, then grasped her bottom with both hands and poised at her entrance.

"Speaking of careful," she said. "We don't have a condom."

"That could be a problem." He was very still, watching her eyes, waiting for her to make the call.

"Or not." She unwrapped her legs from around him and let her feet slide to the sand beneath them. "It just means we have to get creative." She wrapped her hand around his penis and gently squeezed.

He grinned. "I like creative."

He kissed her again, then cupped her breasts in his hands, brushing lightly across her nipples. She fondled his balls with one hand, raking her nails across them, smiling when his breath caught and his eyes lost focus. He widened his stance, bracing himself, and she began to stroke the length of his shaft, exploring the heat and the weight of him, matching her breathing to his own, feeling the tension and need grow within her as it did within him.

He bent his head and drew her left nipple into his mouth, sucking gently at the fabric-covered flesh, stroking with his tongue. She swayed on her feet, rocked both by the waves and the onslaught of sensation. She could feel the muscles of her vagina contracting, her body arched toward him in silent pleading. "I wish you were in me," she whispered.

"I wish I were in you." Then he was in her—not his cock, but his fingers, stroking inside of her while his thumb circled her clit.

One hand on his shoulder, she stroked his penis with the other, her fingers sliding up and down in the lubrication of the warm water, marveling at the erotic contrast of satin-soft flesh against iron-hard tissue. She pressed her forehead to his chest, inhaling his lime aftershave and clean cotton scent mingled with the heady musk of sex and the elemental aroma of the sea. She was floating now—not literally, but figuratively, drifting on an ocean of desire, anchored firmly in his arms.

Her legs began to tremble with the effort of standing, and her hand on him stilled, her whole being poised on the edge of release.

When her climax came, it hit with the force of a mighty wave. Her cries were lost in the sound of the surf, and her hand began to move again in rhythm with the aftershocks that rocked her. She wanted this same feeling for him, this sense of being set loose from gravity to soar, if only for a moment, above anything she'd known before.

He grasped both her shoulders and tensed, coming with a loud cry, his seed mingling with the sea. She continued to stroke until his hand stilled her. He kissed her forehead, her eyes, her lips. "I have a hard time controlling myself around you," he said.

"I know the feeling." She smiled up at him. "It feels good. I'm usually a little *too* in control. At least that's what Candy and Ellie think. It's one reason they talked me into coming on this vacation."

"I'm glad they convinced you to come here, no matter what the reason."

"Yeah, me too." She wasn't going to think about what would happen when the week was over. That was days away yet. Ellie had challenged her to have a fling and so far Sara had succeeded beyond her wildest dreams. Whether it was the beach or the freedom of being away from the office or her resolve to shake up her life a little, things were off to a very good start indeed.

THE SUN was barely up when Sara tiptoed up the steps to the beach house, shoes in hand. She was still wearing Drew's T-shirt, and she had no doubt her hair and her makeup were a mess, but she didn't care. She had never felt so wonderful. So alive.

She and Drew had spent the night walking the beach and talking. They'd discussed everything from favorite foods—his was macaroni and cheese, hers was praline cheesecake—to best childhood Christmas gifts—his was his first surfboard, hers was a pink leather diary with a gold heart-shaped lock and key. They had laughed and kissed and thought of nothing but each other for the whole night.

She was inserting her key in the front-door lock when Candy came up the steps to the deck. She motioned Sara away from the door, grinning. "Looks like you had an interesting night," she whispered. She eyed Sara's T-shirt/minidress with a questioning look. "Wasn't Drew wearing that last night?"

Sara felt her face grow hot. "Yes, it's his." She fished the red halter dress out of her bag. "Thanks so much," she said. "I'll have it cleaned for you."

"No, you won't." Candy accepted the dress and stuffed it into her own bag. "If it helped you end up like that, it's worth every crease. So what happened?"

"It's a long story."

"I've got time."

"And I've got coffee." They looked around and found Ellie standing in the open door wearing an oversize black Siouxsie and the Banshees T-shirt that apparently served as her nightshirt. She held out two cups of coffee. "It's my blend, girls. Come inside and tell me everything. I've got warm ruglah, too."

Moments later, the three friends sat at the kitchen table, savoring some of Ellie's special blend of Guatemalan and Colombian beans and a plate of ruglah from the bakery that supplied Dark Gothic Roast. "So spill, you two," she said. "What have you been up to all night?"

"Who won the hot-shot photo contest?" Sara asked, stalling for time.

"Not us." Ellie made a face. "These two guys and a girl. I don't know how the three of them found everything, but they did."

"I think Drew and I ran into them," Sara said. "The girl was drawing a birthmark on one guy's butt."

"At least we had a *real* birthmark," Candy said. She popped one of the bite-sized pastries into her mouth.

"I thought that looked familiar," Ellie said. "I have a picture of Matt and some friends mooning my girl-friends and me at a slumber party for my ninth birthday that features that birthmark. The question is, how did *you* know it was there?"

Candy grinned and wiped sugar from her lips. "I'll never tell." Her expression sobered. "But I'm sorry we didn't win the contest. We were doing really well, then Matt and I got, um, distracted."

"Same here," Sara said.

Both women looked at her. "Is that Drew's shirt you're wearing?" Ellie asked.

"And have you been in the ocean?" Candy brushed dried salt from Sara's shoulder.

"Yes…and yes." Sara drank the last of her coffee and picked pastry crumbs from the napkin in front of her. She knew the other two were waiting for her to elaborate. "We needed a picture of a woman in a wet T-shirt—for the contest, right?" she said. "So I put on Drew's shirt and went into the ocean and…"

"And one thing led to another." Candy ate another piece of ruglah. "I get the picture."

"So was it amazing? Wonderful? Hot fun?" Ellie leaned toward her.

"It was all those things." *And more.*

"Mmm, sex in the ocean." Ellie licked sugar from her fingers. "What a great first time."

Sara didn't correct her. She didn't want to admit she'd had sex twice in one night to a man she'd known scarcely twenty-four hours.

Candy hugged her. "I'm so proud of you, girl."

"This isn't like me at all," Sara said.

"That's the point of being here—to be different," Candy said.

"Speaking of being different," Ellie said. "It's your turn. Tell us again about how you and Matt will never be a notch on my matchmaker's belt."

"It's actually quite sensible." Candy focused on mashing ruglah crumbs with her forefinger. "We just added sex to our, um, work deal. It's a vacation affair that won't change anything. In fact, right now I'm going to work up a marketing plan I promised to show him later."

"Hold it." Ellie stared at her. "You and my brother made mad hot love last night and this morning you're *working?*" She looked at Sara. "Is she channeling you now?"

"It fits, don't you see?" Candy continued. "What better way to prove to Matt that I can work as hard as I play?"

Sara marveled at her friend. From what little she'd seen of Candy and Matt last night, she had her doubts about them returning to strictly business when they all got back to L.A. But if anyone could pull off such a thing, it would be Candy. Nobody Sara knew played harder, but she still managed to do a great job at the office. If only Sara could juggle the two parts of her own life so well.

Candy not so subtly changed the subject. "We told you our stories, El," she said. "What about you and Bill? How did you two make out?"

"Exactly," she said. "We did make out. On the Ferris wheel. It was so…sexy and…romantic… and…I don't know…."

"That's all you did? Make out?"

"Uh-huh, that's all." She poured more milk into her coffee, stirred, and offered a funny smile. "And who knows what will happen tonight after the shoot. We're getting together."

"We want the full scoop later, don't we, Sara?" Candy said.

While Ellie nibbled the last piece of pastry, Candy pushed her chair back from the table. "I have to get to work now," she said, going to the sofa and firing up the laptop.

Ellie protested, but Candy wouldn't be deterred. Sara left the two of them discussing the matter and headed to her bedroom. She'd only taken a few steps when her phone rang.

"Hello, Uncle Spence," Candy and Ellie chorused as she flipped open the phone.

Sara stuck her tongue out and turned her back to them. "Hello, Uncle Spence… No, you didn't wake me… Of course I can help you." She was back in familiar territory now, her nose to the grindstone. It wasn't as enchanting as wandering the beach all night with a studly guy, but a woman couldn't live on fantasy alone, could she?

"How DID it go yesterday with that chick?" Cooter asked. "The one who wanted surfing lessons."

"Sara?" Drew looked up from the supply catalog he'd been pretending to study. In reality, he hadn't been able to get his mind off Sara and the events of last night. "She's great," he said. He couldn't remember when he'd been so crazy about a woman.

From the moment he'd seen her standing on the deck of the beach house, she'd claimed all his attention. Last night had been the closest he'd ever come to an out-of-body experience. They'd walked the beach for hours, talking about everything, then sat on the pier, watching the sun come up. Only reluctantly had he left her at her beach house, and walked back to his place alone. Now he felt empty, because it had been three hours since he'd seen her.

How much worse was it going to be when she left at the end of the week?

He pushed the thought out of his mind. The point of this whole thing with Sara was to live in the moment. To have the kind of fun he hadn't allowed in his life lately.

"Think you'll make a surfer out of her?" Cooter fished three tubes of sunblock from a bowl on the counter and began juggling them.

A surfer? Oh yeah. He'd forgotten all about that. "Sure," he said. "She has a good sense of balance and she really wants to learn."

"Not bad-looking either." Cooter grinned. "You gonna see her again?"

"I saw her last night." He kept his expression neutral.

"You dog!" Cooter juggled faster, sending the tubes higher into the air. "Did y'all go to that beach festival?"

"Yeah, we checked it out. Were you there?"

"Hell, yeah, I was there." Cooter caught the sunblock and replaced the tubes in the bowl. "I never saw so many half-dressed, drunk women in my life." He laughed. "It was wild."

"Yeah. Pretty wild." *Almost as wild as sex with Sara.* Drew was getting hard again, just thinking about it.

The door opened and Gus shuffled in. Drew stood, alarmed at his grandfather's appearance. Gus's face was ashen, his hair uncombed, his clothes rumpled. "Grandpa, what's wrong?" Drew asked.

Gus waved him away and slumped onto the stool at the end of the counter. "I'm fine," he said. "I was up late partying last night. I'll be fine once I've had some caffeine. Cooter, get me a Dew from the cooler, okay?"

"Sure, Gus." Cooter hurried to retrieve a can of Mountain Dew from the cooler at the back of the shop. He brought it to Gus, along with a granola bar. "You should have some food too," he said.

"Thanks." Gus cracked open the soda and took a long swallow.

"Have you been out all night?" Drew asked. Come to think of it, that was the same shirt and shorts Gus had worn yesterday. "I thought you were playing poker last night."

"I took a rain check. Met up with some folks from the set and we hung out at the festival," Gus said. He smiled wanly. "We were having such a good time we went back to the beach house they'd rented and I crashed there."

"Grandpa! You can't stay out all night like that. You need your rest." Drew frowned. "And you need a decent breakfast, too."

Gus crumpled up the granola bar wrapper and threw it toward the trash can. It bounced off the side and landed on the floor. "I'll go home and rest later," he said. "Don't be such an old woman."

"I wouldn't act like an old woman if you'd behave more like an old man."

"Who are you calling an old man?" Gus glared at him. "Age is all in your head. I don't feel seventy, so why do I have to act seventy?"

Drew shook his head. It was a familiar argument—one he could never win. He was glad Gus wasn't sitting around the house, depressed and lonely, but he wished he would take better care of himself. The next heart attack he had might very well be his last.

Gus took a big bite of granola bar. "Did you go out what that girl last night?" he asked after he'd washed the granola down with more soda. "The one who came by here yesterday afternoon?"

"Her name is Sara and yes, we went out." He closed the supply catalog, giving up all pretense of interest in it.

"They went to that *Sin on the Beach* festival," Cooter said. "Gotta say, that whole spread was radical."

Gus's gaze fixed on Drew. "I thought I saw you there." He grinned. "The two of you were headed toward the old lifeguard shack."

"You dog!" Cooter punched Drew's shoulder. "You didn't waste any time, did you?"

"Shut up." It was true he and Sara hadn't exactly taken things slowly. But the knowledge that she was only here for a few days was always in the back of his mind. He didn't want to waste a single hour.

So what was he doing here when he could be with her on the beach? He glanced at Gus, intending to ask him to watch the store. But the old man's color still wasn't very good. He ought to be home in bed. "Grandpa, why don't you go home and rest," he said. "I can take care of things here."

"I'm fine, dammit." Gus slammed his empty soda can on the counter and stood. "I need to be on the *Sin on the Beach* set in an hour," he said. "I'm going home to take a shower and change. I'll see you two later."

Drew rested his chin in his hands and stared after his grandfather. "What am I going to do with him, Cooter?" he asked. "He refuses to take care of himself."

"You know what they say," Cooter said. "It's better to burn out than fade away."

"I don't want Gus doing either one."

The phone rang and he answered it. "The Surf Shack. This is Drew."

"Drew, honey, I just called to see how things are going." His mother still sounded like a young girl on the phone, full of energy and optimism, like the woman herself.

"Hi, Mom. I'm fine. How are things in Arizona?"

"Hot!" She laughed. "But you know we love it. The shop has been so busy we're thinking about hiring help. And your father is going to a trade show in Prescott next week."

"That's great." Though his parents had moved intending to retire, they hadn't been there a month before they'd purchased a storefront and opened a business that catered to the rock hounds who frequented the area. They thrived on the challenge of running a business and would probably never stop working.

"How is your grandfather?" his mom asked.

"He's doing well. There's a beach festival here this week, from that television show, *Sin on the Beach.* They're filming some episodes and Grandpa got hired as an extra."

His mother laughed. "Oh, he must love that! Imagine, taking up acting at his age."

"I think he's mainly playing himself, but he enjoys it," Drew said. "I just hope they don't wear him out."

"I'm trusting you to make sure he gets his rest," his mother said. "And how are things at the Surf Shack? I imagine you're busy with this festival going on."

"Yeah, pretty busy."

"Thank God you're there to keep things going and help Gus out," she said. "It makes me sick every time I think he might have had to close the place. I have so many happy memories of it—I can't imagine it not being there."

"Yeah." He had a lot of memories of this store himself.

"Did you get that new shipment of boards your grandfather was talking about ordering?" she continued.

"Yeah, we did."

She moved on to asking about Cooter, and the rest of the inventory, still interested in all the details of the shop even though she'd been away for several years. "You haven't asked what I've been up to," he said, interrupting her.

"I imagine you're looking after your grandfather, surfing and running the Surf Shack," she said. "Is there something else?"

No, that's my life, he thought. Or it had been until two days ago. "I met a girl," he said.

"Ohhh." The single vowel was drawn out like a distant siren's wail. "A surfer?"

"I'm giving her lessons."

"Well, tell me about her. How did you meet? How long have you been seeing her?"

"We met on the beach. Two days ago."

He sensed his mother's interest fading as soon as she realized this romance was brand-new. "That's nice, dear. I'm glad you're getting out and meeting other young people. Is your grandfather there? I'd like to talk to him."

"He went home to get cleaned up, then he was going over to the television-show set."

"Then I'll call him later. I have to go now. You take care."

"You, too, Mom."

He hung up and stared at the phone, not really seeing it. Instead, he was picturing his mother, her blond hair pulled back in a ponytail, a bathing suit under her T-shirt and shorts, ready to hit the waves at any opportunity. She was her father's daughter, and her life was the Surf Shack and her family. Strange to think of her now as an Arizona rock hound, but she seemed to love it. And as long as she could call and get regular updates on how the Surf Shack and everyone there was doing, she seemed happy.

Though he would have been happier if she'd asked about him first and the Surf Shack second.

He moved out from behind the counter. "I'm going out for a while," he said to Cooter. "Call me on my cell if it gets too busy for you."

"No problem." Cooter leaned back against the counter. "Say hello to Sara for me."

"What makes you think I'm going to see Sara?" he asked, annoyed.

Cooter laughed. "If I'd spent last night with a chick like that, I know *I'd* be going to see her again. Besides, I can't think of another reason you'd leave the shop in the middle of the day."

"I just need to get out of here for a while," he said. "I'm going for a walk." And if the walk happened to take him by a certain beach house, maybe he'd stop in and say hello. But mainly, he needed time to clear his head and try to figure out what to do about his grandfather.

It was one thing to champion the carefree live-for-today, never-worry-about-tomorrow surfer lifestyle, but the time came when a man had to put that aside. If Gus didn't start worrying about his future he likely wouldn't have one. And Drew didn't miss the irony that he was giving up a large part of his freedom to do Gus's worrying for him.

"SARA, I need you to call Phil Metterly right away and explain to him why his closing was changed from this Friday to next Friday." Uncle Spence sounded out of breath. Frantic.

"The closing was delayed because the title insurance policy couldn't be issued in time," she said. "You could have told him that."

"But he wants to hear it from you. You're supposed to be handling this account. He says he's going to find someone else to handle his business unless he gets the answers to his questions right away." His voice rose with each new sentence, until he practically spoke in a falsetto.

"I'll call him," Sara said. "Calm down."

"Thank you." She heard him inhale deeply, then let out the breath in a rush. Probably something his new golf pro had taught him. Sara wasn't the only one who was always after Spence to relax. "I knew I could count on you," he said.

That was her—always dependable. Calm in any crisis. Except, right now she felt irritated. Uncle Spence could have found the information, if he'd wanted to. He wasn't dumb. And he'd run the business by himself for years before she came along. "I'll call Mr. Metterly and talk to him." She knew how to handle Metterly's type—stay calm, apologize and add flattery if necessary. With most people the problem wasn't so much that they weren't getting their way as it was that they felt no one was acknowledging their problem. They wanted to know that you cared and you weren't blowing them off.

"I miss the old days sometimes," Spence said. "When I never had to deal with people like him. I did mostly small residential closings back then. Not as much money in it as the business we have these days, but the people were nicer. Young couples happy to be in their first homes, retirees starting over in a new place—I felt as if all my customers were my friends. I never feel that when I'm dealing with some big corporation or conglomerate."

The familiar pinch of guilt hurt her stomach. "I thought you liked the new business I brought in," she said. It had been her idea to go after corporate clients. She'd seen an under-served niche and her gamble had paid off. In a few short years Anderson Title had grown from a one-man concern to one of the top title companies in the region.

"I do!" he said. "You've done a wonderful job building the business. I never could have grown this much on my own. You've made me rich." He sighed. "But now that I'm older, sometimes I miss dealing with those smaller accounts."

"Maybe we should consider opening a small-account division," she said. There wasn't much money in it, but if it kept Uncle Spence happy and out of her hair she was all for it.

"I don't know about that." His voice resumed its usual briskness. "Just call Metterly and calm him down."

"I will." She started to say goodbye, but his next question surprised her.

"How is your vacation going?"

"Great." She smiled, glad to talk about something other than work. "I'm learning to surf." *And I met this great guy.*

"I remember when you used to hang out with all

those surfers on County Line Beach," he said. "It wasn't a good crowd. Your mother worried about you all the time. I did, too."

"It's not like that, Uncle Spence," she said. "Nothing like that at all." She knew he was picturing the times she'd come home from a day at the beach, in a daze from smoking pot or drinking all day, sullen and argumentative. She'd skip school, shoplift, break curfew—anything that felt like rebelling. She'd thought she was lashing out against the rules and authority that oppressed her, but in reality she'd been trying to blot out the pain and misery within her. She'd missed her father. She'd missed her old life in Georgia. She'd felt as if she didn't fit in in California, and that she never would.

"Malibu isn't like County Line Beach," she said. "The people here aren't like the people I hung out with then." *Drew isn't like any man I've ever known.* "And I'm not like that anymore either. You know that. You took me away from all that and helped me turn my life around."

"You didn't need that much help," he said gruffly. "Just a little guidance."

"I'll never forget what you did for me back then," she said. "I owe you so much."

"Just call Metterly for me, hon. I'd better go now. I have a tee time at noon."

"Bye, Uncle Spence. I love you."

"I love you, too, sweetie."

While searching for Phil Metterly's number, she pulled up the pictures Drew had taken of her last night. There she was, standing in the ocean wearing his T-shirt, the wet fabric clinging to her body. She looked wild and uninhibited. Sexy and alluring. Her best fantasy of herself.

She squeezed her thighs together at the memory of their lovemaking in the water. It had been a moment out of time, primitive and erotic, forging a connection between them that went beyond the mere physical.

Would such intense emotion survive the bright light of day? After all, fantasies were the stuff of dreams. Not meant to be real or to fit in with the responsibilities of work and family and everyday life.

Yet Drew was definitely a flesh-and-blood person, not a figment of her imagination. And all she wanted right now was to see him again.

But first, she had to work. She had to be responsible and take care of business. Maybe, like Candy, she could learn to balance work and play. But at this moment she was a one-thing-at-a-time kind of woman.

She got Phil Metterly on the phone and succeeded in charming him into a better frame of mind. She pointed out he'd locked in his interest rate and that he had nothing to worry about from the delayed closing. By the end of the conversation, he was actually laughing and joking with her. She hung up the phone and sighed. If only all her problems were that easy to handle.

For now, a shower and a change of clothes would definitely take care of the problem of her appearance. When she saw her reflection in the bathroom mirror, she had to stifle a scream. What makeup that wasn't deposited beneath her eyes had washed off completely, and her hair resembled a fright wig.

A shower, blow dry and reapplication of makeup later, she was dressed in clean shorts and a shirt, considering hitting the kitchen for a snack.

"Sara! Someone here to see you!" Candy called.

She left her room and found Drew standing in the doorway leading onto the deck. He, too, had changed into a fresh shirt and board shorts—both blue. There were faint circles under his eyes, but they only added a sleepy seductiveness to his already tempting looks. "Ready for another surfing lesson?" he asked.

"Let me change into my swimsuit and I'll be right out."

In record time she donned a black and red-flowered tankini, stuffed a cover-up and her phone into her bag and joined him on the deck. They waved goodbye to Candy and headed down the beach.

When they were out of sight of the beach house, Drew stopped and pulled her into his arms. "I've been dying to kiss you again," he said.

"And I've been waiting to be kissed." She smiled. "Candy wouldn't have minded."

"I'll remember that next time."

Then they didn't talk for a while, reveling in a kiss that was every bit as intoxicating as a whole bottle of wine for Sara. She was tempted to suggest they forget the surfing lesson and spend the afternoon in bed, but she had the tournament to prepare for, and Candy and Ellie were counting on her to win points for the team. "We'd better get to that lesson," she said.

They stopped by the Surf Shack and collected two boards. Cooter saluted them from behind the counter, where he was discussing the merits of various rash guards with a customer.

"Where's your grandfather today?" Sara asked as they left the shop.

"Doing something on the set of that television show." Drew frowned. "He was out all night with people from the show. When he came in this morning, he was positively gray. He should be home in bed, resting."

"He's amazing," she said. "And I'll bet he's really excited about being on the show. I know Ellie is."

"Grandpa just likes being involved in things. He wants to be wherever the action is, even if it's somewhere he doesn't belong."

"I'm sure when he gets too tired, he'll take a break," she tried to reassure him. "After all, at his age, he has to slow down some time."

"That's what I keep thinking, but the only thing that's slowed him down so far are his two heart attacks. And even then, he didn't take it easy for long." He glanced at her, worry making deep lines on his forehead. "I'm afraid next time he might stop altogether."

She squeezed his arm. "It's hard when you feel responsible. Believe me, I know."

His eyes met hers. "You do know, don't you? I think that's one of the things I love most about you. You don't just say you understand—you really *do* understand."

Her vision grew fuzzy as she listened to his words, though much of what he said after *love* didn't register. Did Drew love her? Was it even possible to love someone you'd only just met?

Oh God. She didn't *even* want to go there. This was supposed to be a fling. A fun few days. Couldn't she do *anything* anymore without getting serious?

7

"TODAY we're going to work more on standing up on the board," Drew said once they'd reached the water's edge. "Then we'll move on to angling across the wave." He planted his board in the sand and pointed to a wave headed toward shore. "If you angle along the face of the wave, parallel to the beach, instead of coming straight in, you'll get a longer ride and have more fun."

She nodded. "So you're really riding the wave, not just letting it push you to shore."

"Exactly!" He was watching the wave, as he'd watched thousands of other waves, measuring the distance between swells, judging the height and the time before it broke, imagining how he would approach it, what angle he would take to ride it. But all the while another part of him was aware of Sara standing so close beside him. He smelled the orange-and-vanilla scent of her hair and heard the soft sigh of each exhalation of her breath. The wind blew a strand of hair across one eye and he wanted to brush it away for her, to feel the satin of her cheek beneath his fingers.

And then she was looking at him, a question in her eyes. "What do we do next?" she asked.

All right, bro, get your mind back on the business at hand. "Grab your board and let's get out there."

They paddled out to the waves. He was pleased to see she remembered what he'd told her about duck diving. He chose a section of shore with smaller waves and not many people, and had her practice standing on the board over and over, each time riding it to the shallows or until she fell.

Before long, she wasn't falling at all, and could stay on the board for longer periods. They graduated to larger waves, and began to practice angling. "First you have to decide which direction you want to move—left or right," Drew explained. "With smaller waves like this, you want to start angling about halfway up the face of the wave."

"I get that," she said. "But how do you turn a surfboard?"

"That's the easiest part. You just look in the direction you want to go and lean very slightly to that side. Don't lean too far or you'll go over. Always keep your body centered over the board. And remember, in surfing, speed is your friend. The faster you're moving, the easier everything is."

"Easy for you," she chided. But she turned her board and began paddling out, waiting for the next set of waves.

He hung back, paddling gently to stay in place, and watched her take the wave. She started angling a little too soon, shortening the time of her ride, but for a first effort, it was good. She was getting more comfortable on the board, instinctively finding her balance.

She paddled over to him and he shared this assessment. "A few more days of practice and you'll be in good shape for the competition. In your class the judges won't be looking for a lot of fancy maneuvers, just a good understanding of the basics."

"I really want to do well," she said. "To win. Candy's already won tons of points between the limbo contest and a karaoke contest. She's really amazing. The woman never met a stranger and she really knows how to have fun."

"I've had a lot of fun with you." He waggled his eyebrows in an exaggerated leer.

She laughed. "I'm good with you, but Candy can have fun with anyone. Everyone likes her. And Ellie's in the TV show. She's just so—*stylish*. You saw her with the makeover we did for the show, but ordinarily she's very goth—black hair, black nails, very cutting-edge fashion. Goth, but with a real glamour-girl twist. And she's so nice. She's always looking after everyone. I think everyone in our building goes to her for help with their problems."

"Your friends sound great," he said. "But you're great, too." Why didn't she give herself more credit? "You're caring and fun and sexy." He hugged her to him. "And you're turning out to be a halfway decent surfer."

She laughed and turned toward him to kiss him. Soon they were making out in the water again and he wondered if they were on their way to a repeat of the previous night.

But the drone of a motorboat interrupted them. Sara looked around, then Drew directed her attention overhead. "Parasailers," he said.

She looked up and watched the bright red, blue, yellow and green parachute draw nearer. When it was almost overhead, they could make out a man and a woman beneath the sail. The woman's brown hair streamed out behind her and she wore a bright-yellow bikini beneath a yellow life jacket.

"That's Candy!" Sara waved, but already the sail had turned away. "It's Candy and Matt." She grinned. "I'm glad to see she didn't spend *all* day working." Shading her eyes, she watched the bright parachute until it disappeared from sight, then turned to Drew, her eyes aglow. "I told you Candy would do anything."

"Do you want to go parasailing?" he asked. The thought of being snugged in a harness next to her was appealing.

She shook her head. "I could never do something so daring."

"Why not? Learning to surf isn't exactly sitting on the beach building sand castles," he said. "It takes guts."

"I guess I don't think of myself as very daring." She shrugged. "I used to be, but taking risks got me into trouble, so I started playing it safe."

She'd hinted before about her troubled past, but seemed reluctant to elaborate. Was it because she thought he'd think less of her? He smoothed her hair back from her face. "I can't believe you were ever that bad," he said.

She looked away from him. "I guess it could have been worse," she said. "I didn't end up in jail or anything, though I could have. But I did stupid stuff—hung out with a rough crowd, gang members and thugs, drug dealers and dropouts and street people. I skipped school and did drugs and drank. I thought I was so mature and independent. I gave my mom a lot of grief she didn't need."

He put his hand under her chin and tilted her head until she was looking him in the eye. "But you wised up and straightened your life out. Your mom must be really proud of you for that."

"I'd never have done it without Uncle Spence," she said. "He got tired of listening to my mom cry about all the trouble I was getting into, so one day he came down to the beach and got me. He took me to his house and literally locked me in a room, and told me he was in charge now. I wasn't allowed to go anywhere without him, I couldn't talk on the phone or see any of my old friends. He hired a tutor to come to the house to catch me up on my school-work and in the afternoons I had to work in his office."

"That's really tough love," Drew said.

She nodded. "At first I hated him. I screamed and cried and threatened to call the police and tell them I'd been kidnapped. Then he showed me a piece of paper my mom had written, giving him permission to take charge of me." She smiled. "I figured out later it wasn't a legal document or anything, but it was enough to convince me that I had to do what he said. And I think even then, when I was so angry, part of me was grateful. He'd taken me out of that scene. There were times I'd been truly scared—times when I realized I was out there all alone with some pretty rough people who'd done bad things. It was exciting, but I always knew in the back of my mind that it was dangerous. I just didn't know how to get out of the life I'd gotten myself into."

"So his approach worked." Drew tried to imagine her as a silly, scared teenager. At first he couldn't see it. The woman before him was so calm, so capable, so together. But then she looked into his eyes again, and somewhere in those green-gold depths he glimpsed the fear and insecurity the years had not quite erased.

She nodded. "After a few months I quit pouting and started to enjoy myself. I made friends in the neighborhood, and I really liked working for Uncle Spence. Back then, Anderson Title was a small company that specialized in residential real estate transactions. After I graduated high school I took courses at night at the local community college and eventually earned my degree in business. I suggested we try to go after some bigger contracts and commercial real estate. From there the business really took off."

"The tough guy who pulled you off the streets doesn't sound like a man who'd be easily overwhelmed," Drew said.

"Not overwhelmed, exactly," she said. "But he

expects a lot from me and I worry about disappointing him. And, too, as he gets older, I don't think he handles change as well."

"Maybe that's part of my grandpa's problem—he doesn't like the idea of changing his lifestyle for his health."

"Maybe so." She hugged him. "Talking about all this with you makes me feel better. Thanks."

"I know what you mean," he said. "Everything seems better when I'm with you." He kissed her lightly on the forehead, not wanting to start anything more right now. It was enough to be with her this way, sharing a love of the ocean and the intimacy of exchanged confidences.

"Let's take a break," he said. "Neither of us got much sleep last night and I don't want to overdo it. Staying in the water too long when you're tired is a recipe for trouble."

She stifled a yawn. "I don't know why you think I'm tired."

She laughed and they paddled toward shore. They had scarcely stood on the sand when he heard the tinny notes of "Bolero." "Is that your phone?" he asked.

She groaned. "Want to bet it's Uncle Spence?"

"It might be one of your roommates," he said.

She checked the phone and shook her head. "I'll call him back later." She looked at him. "I really should go back to the beach house and see to a few things," she said.

"Yeah. I should get back to the shop and help

Cooter. He's probably swamped." But he had no enthusiasm for the idea. "Tell you what," he said. "Let's get together this evening, after the shop closes. I'll take you to dinner. You like seafood?"

She smiled. "I love seafood."

"Great. I'll stop by the beach house about six-thirty. Sound good?"

"It sounds great." They walked up the beach to the turnoff to her rental. "I'll take your board back to the shop," he said. "See you this evening."

She kissed him on the lips and it was all he could do not to drop the surfboards and pull her close. "I can't wait," she said, with a heated look.

One more night together. One more night closer to when she would leave. He shook his head, refusing to think about that. All that mattered was that he'd get to spend a few more hours with Sara. He'd do everything he could to make the most of that time, to make it an evening neither one of them would ever forget.

NOT WANTING to borrow from Candy's wardrobe again, Sara wore the one good dress she'd packed, a simple white sheath, which she dressed up with a double strand of coral beads she'd found at a souvenir shop on the beach. When she stepped out of her bedroom, both Ellie and Candy whistled. "You look great," Ellie said. "Are you going somewhere special?"

"Drew's taking me out for seafood."

"A real dinner date?" Candy looked up from where she was painting her toenails fire-engine red. "This sounds serious."

"It's not serious." She fiddled with the beads, the rough coral sliding back and forth through her fingers. "I mean, it's a vacation fling, right?"

"But sometimes flings turn into something more," Ellie said. "At least, that's what I hear."

"I didn't come here looking for something more," Sara said. "I mean, I just want to have fun. To prove I don't have to be serious all the time."

"So have a fun, not-serious dinner," Candy said.

"I really like Drew." Sara sat on the edge of the sofa-bed, hands knotted in her lap. "He understands about my work and Uncle Spence and everything. He even has some of the same problems, running his surfing shop and looking after his grandfather."

"If it's meant to be, you'll find a way to work it out," Ellie said.

Easy for Ellie to say. She had such an easygoing, positive approach to life. But Sara had more doubts. Right now, she was having a hard time picturing her life without Drew in it. But was it the idea of going back to being celibate that she shied away from? Or a true reluctance to part from a man who had already come to mean so much to her?

"What happens in Malibu stays in Malibu," Candy said. She switched to the nails on her other foot. "It's why vacation romances are so exciting and intense—everything's compressed into a short amount of time. But it's hard to carry that into the real world."

"I don't want to think about any of that right now," Sara said. "I just want to enjoy being with

Drew." Would things have been different if they'd met in Los Angeles? Their relationship likely wouldn't have progressed so quickly. They might have gone on a few dates—if they could each juggle their schedules to allow that. Eventually they would have slept together—probably sooner rather than later, if the intensity of their attraction to each other was any indication. But they wouldn't have had hours of free time to get to know each other as they had so far.

He was truly amazing. Would she have seen that if he had been a client who tried to date her, or a man she met during one of her infrequent nights on the town with friends? Certainly he wouldn't resent her heavy work schedule the way some of the men she'd dated before had. After all, he had responsibilities of his own.

A horn honked and Sara stood and looked out to see Drew, in a red-and-white Mustang convertible. He parked in front of the house and got out. She met him at the door. "Hey, there," she said, grinning at him. He looked good enough to eat, dressed in an open-collar sports shirt, chinos and leather sandals.

"Love your car," Candy said. She and Ellie came to stand behind Sara in the doorway.

"You remember Candy and Ellie, don't you, Drew?" Sara said.

"Of course." He smiled at them, then turned to Sara. "You ready to go?"

He escorted her down the walk and opened the passenger door for her. "It really is a great car," she said, smoothing her hand along the leather upholstery.

"It was a gift from Grandpa Gus when I graduated college."

"He has good taste."

"He does that." He glanced at her. "He really likes you, after all."

This information surprised her. "But he doesn't even know me," she said. "We only talked for a few minutes that one time at the Surf Shack."

"He says he's a good judge of people." He glanced at her. "Or maybe he's going by how I feel about you."

And how do you feel about me? she wondered. But she wasn't bold enough to ask.

They turned onto a shell road leading to a more rundown neighborhood near the beach. A few minutes later, Drew parked the Mustang in front of a weathered, low-slung building. Vestiges of blue paint were still visible in spots, and a faded sign identified this as The Oyster Bucket. Sara stared, trying to find an appropriate comment.

"I know it looks like a dive," Drew said. "But the food is great. And the owners are friends of mine."

The inside definitely looked more promising, with blue vinyl booths, blond wood tables and captain's chairs. A large woman with amazingly orange hair greeted Drew by name when they entered, and showed them to a booth next to a window. "I'm Large Marge and I've known this fellow since he was still wet behind the ears," she said to Sara. "If you need the skinny on him, you just ask me." She handed them each a plastic-covered menu. "The crab's on special tonight and we're out of oysters."

When they were alone again, Sara leaned across the table and whispered. "Large Marge?"

He laughed. "One of the regulars called her that one day and I guess she liked it because she's called herself that ever since. She and her husband, Del, own this place. I worked here when I was in high school and halfway through college."

Over fried shrimp and scallops, coleslaw and baked potatoes with everything, she learned about his years in college and short-lived career as a claims adjuster for a large insurance company.

"But where does the surfing fit in?" she asked.

"I've been surfing practically since I could walk," he said. "Gus owned the Surf Shack and my parents helped run the place until they retired to Arizona. I literally grew up in that store. Our whole life revolved around it. Gus was my hero. He taught me to surf and gave me my first board."

"For Christmas. I remember you told me." Was it only last night that they'd spent the night walking the beach and talking?

"Even after I went to college I'd surf on weekends and during school break," he said. "By then my grandmother had died and Grandpa was managing the business by himself. My second year in college, he had his first heart attack, but my parents didn't want to upset me, so they played it down. I figured he was doing all right after that—well enough that my parents moved to Arizona and turned the shop over to him."

He took a long sip of water. "Then one day, after

I'd started working at the insurance company, my mom called and told me he was in the hospital. The doctor had called her and she and dad were on their way from Arizona, but I could get to Grandpa a lot sooner."

"That must have been scary," she said. She'd stopped eating and was watching him, studying the play of emotions across his face.

"I couldn't believe it," he said. "I went to see him and didn't even recognize him at first. How could that little old man in that hospital gown be my Grandpa Gus? I always thought of him as so young—just another dude on a surfboard, you know? Seeing him so pale and so—so *silent* was like learning the truth about Santa Claus."

"Is that when you decided to leave your job and work at the Surf Shack?"

"Not right then." He took a long sip of iced tea. "One day my mom pulled me aside and told me that if I didn't come in and take over, Gus would have to sell the business. It was too much for him to handle anymore, but he wouldn't admit it. I saw they were right, but I knew if Gus had to give up the Surf Shack, he'd die. So I offered to come in with him and take over the day-to-day running of the place. He could take it easy and not have to worry about anything." He grimaced. "The trouble is, Gus doesn't know the meaning of *take it easy*."

"So we're both kind of in the same boat," she said. "People we love depend on us to keep things going and we don't want to let them down."

"Yeah, but lately I've been thinking something's got to give."

The way he looked at her, as if he were trying to see down into her soul, made her shiver. "Why is that?" she asked.

"Because…because it seems like the *only* thing in my life is surfing—the business, Gus, even how I spend my spare time. My whole life has been that way." His eyes met hers, his expression troubled. "When I was a kid everything in our family revolved around surfing and the store. I told myself my life would be different—I'd always surf, but I'd have other things going on. I want to have fun in my life again, and I want someone to have fun with."

She thought of the longing that had led to her taking this vacation—the desire to rediscover the strong, carefree girl she'd been. "I'd like more fun in my life, too," she said. "It's one reason I'm here now. And I don't want to spend the rest of my life alone." She swallowed hard. "But I don't know how to manage it all—the business, Uncle Spence and my own happiness."

"Then that's what we need to figure out," he said. "And soon, while we're still young enough to enjoy ourselves."

They finished eating in silence, as if the weight of all they'd said up till now made further conversation seem frivolous. When he'd paid the check and they were back in his car, he put the key in the ignition, but didn't start the engine. "Come back to my place with me," he said.

She knew he was asking for more than a brief stop in for coffee. "What about Gus?" she asked.

"When I left he was in bed. He'll be out for the night." He reached across the seat and took her hand in his. "I want to spend the night with you. All night."

She nodded. "I'd like that too."

His place turned out to be a modest bungalow with gray siding, large windows and decks and a view of the beach. "Gus has an apartment in what used to be the garage," Drew explained after he'd parked the car in the drive. "I live upstairs and we share the kitchen and living room downstairs."

Inside, everything was neater than she'd expected from two bachelors, furnished in comfortable leather and wood furniture, with framed vintage surfing posters on the walls.

"Would you like a drink?" he asked, tossing his car keys onto the bar in the upstairs den.

"No." She set her purse on an end table and turned to him. "All I want is you."

"I like a woman who knows what she wants." He pulled her into his arms and kissed her, lips and tongue and hands letting her know he wanted her as much as she wanted him.

All their talk of the past today had reminded Sara not only of the bad things she was glad to have left behind her, but of the good she'd abandoned along the way. When she was a teenager spending her days on the beach, she'd had the fearlessness of youth, the belief that anything she did would work out all right. She wanted to recapture that part of herself. To leave behind, at least for one night, the mature woman weighted down by responsibility and rediscover the wild child she was sure still lurked within her.

She broke off the kiss and took both his hands in hers. "Where's your bedroom?" she asked.

"Back this way." He pulled her down the hall, to a room furnished only with a double bed, a dresser and a TV on a stand. "The set designers from *Sin on the Beach* haven't asked to recreate this room for the show, for some reason," he joked.

"That's all right." She turned and unfastened the top button of his shirt. "All I'm interested in is the bed and it looks fine."

"Mmm." He reached up to help her, but she batted his hands away. "You just sit over there on the edge. I'm in charge now."

He hesitated, his hands hovering above her shoulders, then he let them drop to his side. "Okay. Whatever you want." He settled onto the bed, his gaze fixed on her.

She smiled at him, a coy look filtered through slightly lowered lashes. "I told you, I want you," she said,

She took her time with the buttons, letting her fingernails scrape his skin as she undid each one. She kissed each section of his chest that was exposed, running her tongue over his skin, tasting it, exploring the texture of the fine dusting of hair, flicking her tongue across one nipple and feeling it tighten and grow more erect. She leaned far forward as she worked so that he had a clear view of the valley between her breasts. She liked thinking about him watching her, imagining him even more aroused by the sight and feel of her, every sensation heightened by the anticipation of what was still to come

The last button undone, she bent and kissed his navel, circling it with her tongue, then laying a wet trail along the line of hair disappearing into the waistband of his chinos. While she did this, he leaned over and lowered the zipper on the back of her dress, and slipped it from her shoulders.

She straightened and backed away. "You aren't very patient, are you?" she teased.

"I want to see you naked." His gaze swept over her, and she imagined she felt heat everywhere he looked. She hooked her thumb over the waistband of her panties. "Would you like me to take these off?" she asked.

"Oh, yes."

She shook her head. "You'll have to wait a little bit longer." Then she stepped forward once more and pushed the shirt off his shoulders, and unfastened the button at the waistband of his chinos. She slipped her hand inside and felt the head of his penis brushing her fingertips. She looked into his eyes as she stroked him lightly. His eyes were very dark, pupils dilated, lids at half-mast. She'd never known before what people meant when they talked about "bedroom eyes."

"It's never taken me this long to get undressed before," he said.

"Some things are best enjoyed slowly." She

lowered the zipper of his pants, one tooth at a time, all the while watching his eyes, the tension coiling tighter and tighter inside her.

At last she pulled down his pants, and the boxers with them, then crouched in front of him. His erection strained toward her and again she felt the thrill of knowing how much he wanted her.

She took him in her mouth, sliding her lips slowly down the length of his shaft, reveling in the silken heat of him. He rocked forward, silently encouraging her, and threaded his fingers through her hair.

She quickened her pace, her breath coming faster in time with his. She teased and sucked and caressed his balls, feeling them tighten as his arousal intensified.

Knowing he was close to coming made her own need even greater. She slid her hand down to stroke herself, and he groaned and dug his fingers into her skin. She felt wild and wanton, powerful and at the same time enslaved by physical passion. Drew was both the catalyst and creator of these feelings. She felt connected to him in some fundamental way that transcended words.

He came like the crash of a wave on the shore, and she tasted his salty-sea essence. Then he pulled her to her feet and urged her to the bed. They lay side by side, entwined, looking into each other's eyes. "I've felt things with you I've never felt with anyone before," he said. "It's more than sex, it's—"

"Shhh." She silenced him with a finger to his lips, then pulled his head down to her breast. She didn't want to analyze her feelings right now, she only wanted to experience them.

While he suckled first one breast and then the other, his fingers parted the folds of her sex and slid inside her, his thumb playing across her clit, making her gasp and writhe beneath him. "Did you catch the big wave?" he murmured, kissing the sensitive skin at the base of her throat. "Ride it. Ride it all the way to shore."

She rode the wave, farther and higher than she had ridden before, and when she climaxed he was there with her, holding her in his arms, cradling her to him as she returned to earth.

They smiled at each other, sated and silly in the afterglow of their lovemaking. "You sure know how to undress a guy," he said.

"I noticed you were fighting me all the way." She snuggled closer. She never wanted this week to end, never wanted to spend another night away from him. Was this what it was like to be in love? When in the past few days had she gone from being intrigued by a man on a surfboard to being unable to think of her life without him in it? Had her feelings morphed from friendship to devotion sometime in the early hours of this morning as they walked the beach? Or had something within her known immediately that Drew was the man for her?

The idea made her a little breathless. If only she had some idea of what he was feeling for her—if she was the only crazy person in this bed right now. She wet her lips and struggled to come up with the right words. "These last few days have been…really special," she said.

"Yeah." He squeezed her tighter against him. "Really special." He rolled to her and brought his lips to hers. As they kissed, she felt she might soar right up to the ceiling if he weren't holding her so tightly. *Keep holding on,* she would have said if she could speak. *Keep holding me and don't you dare let go.*

8

FOR THE first time in memory, Sara woke the next morning without a to-do today list scrolling through her head. The anxiety that drove her from bed each day was gone, replaced by a deep sense of contentment. She and Drew had made love through the night, finally falling asleep in the early-morning hours. She stretched and yawned, luxuriating in the feeling of well-used muscles and a deep satisfaction she had not known before.

In the bed beside her, completely buried beneath the covers, was a man-size lump she assumed was Drew. As she watched, he snored softly, the covers rising and falling gently with each breath. She debated cuddling up to him and coaxing him awake, but he looked so peaceful she decided not to wake him. Moving as quietly as possible, she slipped out of bed and into the bathroom.

Dressed in the clothes she'd worn the night before, she made her way downstairs, toward the beckoning scent of coffee.

Gus stood in front of the stove, an apron that said Kiss the Cook tied around his ample waist. "I hope you're hungry," he said by way of greeting. "I'm making pancakes. Coffee's next to the sink."

He acted as if finding her here this morning was the most natural thing in the world, so she followed his lead and made herself at home. She found a mug and filled it from the carafe in the coffeemaker, then sat at the table. "Can I do anything to help?" she asked.

"Nope. I do most of the cooking around here. I know my way around the kitchen and I prefer to take care of things myself." He expertly flipped a pair of pancakes. "I supposed my grandson is sleeping in."

"He was asleep when I left. I didn't have the heart to wake him."

"Hmph. When I was his age, I was up early every morning. You miss some of the best wave action if you stay in bed half the day." He turned and set a plate of steaming flapjacks in front of her. "Help yourself to the butter and syrup. And don't give me any guff about being on a diet. If you're going to spend all day in the surf, you need some good carbs."

"Yes sir." Smiling to herself, she slathered butter between the pancakes and poured on the syrup. By the time she picked up her fork, he'd joined her at the table, his own plate filled.

They ate in silence for a while, Sara pausing between bites to study her surroundings, like an anthropologist searching for clues as to the lifestyle of a new species. The room was white—enamel cabinets, countertops, tile. The only color came from a set of bright-red canisters, red-and-white checked curtains at the window and the red oven mitts Gus had been using while he cooked.

"Don't let the neatness fool you," Gus said when he had emptied his plate. "We have a cleaning service come in once a week. They were here yesterday."

"Have you lived in this house a long time?" she asked.

"Since 1974. After my wife passed, I moved downstairs. It felt more comfortable that way. After I had my second heart attack and Drew started working at the Surf Shack, he moved in upstairs. He said it was so he could be close to work and save money on rent, but I know it's because he wants to keep an eye on me."

"He loves you very much," she said.

Gus nodded. "I know. You can never win an argument with someone who loves you that way, did you know that? No matter what you say, they're always going to be convinced they have your best interests at heart. There's no room for compromise with that kind of love."

"You make it sound like a bad thing," she said.

He stood and carried their plates to the sink. "No, it's not a bad thing. It is what it is. Absolutes of any kind are hard to deal with—absolute love, absolute hate, absolute power, absolute devotion to an ideal."

"Drew didn't tell me you were a philosopher."

"I'm a surfer." He began rinsing the plates and loading them into the dishwasher. "You have a lot of time to think out there on the water."

"All I can think about when I'm out there is trying to stay on the surfboard," she confessed.

He chuckled. "How are the surfing lessons coming?"

"Sometimes I feel like I've really got the hang of it." She shook her head. "Other times I think I'll never be any good."

"So why did you choose surfing?" He shut the dishwasher and turned to study her. "Why not play pool or do the limbo or freak dance or something?"

A fair question, she supposed. "When I was a teenager, I spent a lot of time on the beach watching surfers. I always wanted to be one of them. They looked so…free."

He nodded. "My grandson tells me you're doing well—that you have a good sense of balance and you're not afraid."

If only those words applied to her real life! The thought startled her. It was true she wasn't very balanced in her daily life—everyone knew she worked too much. She knew it herself. As for fear…maybe that was the real thing that drove her. Fear of disappointing someone. Fear of screwing up. "Do you have any idea who my competition will be?" she asked. "Are they any good?"

"I hope you're not trying to influence a judge." He looked stern, but the laughter in his eyes gave him away.

"I wouldn't think of it," she said, then changed the subject back to her chief interest of the moment. "Drew told me he worked as an insurance adjuster before he decided to help you with the Surf Shack," she said.

"Why he ever took a job like that in the first place is beyond me. That boy was made to be out doing things, being on the water, not stuck in a cubicle, chained to a desk."

She nodded. "You're right. I don't think he'd be happy in an office job." Drew had an energy about him she couldn't imagine would mix well in a regimented office environment.

"Surfing is in his blood," Gus said. "The Surf Shack will be his when I'm gone—that was my plan all along, but I'm glad he's getting the chance to get to know the business while I'm still here to answer his questions."

"I'm sure he works very hard. He told me he puts in some long hours."

Gus frowned. "I tried to get him to hire someone to do the books, but he didn't think we could afford it. He worries about things like that all the time."

"That's part of being a good business person," she said. "Worrying about the bottom line."

"He ought to worry about his *life* instead."

"We have to work to be able to afford a life," she said. "And he feels obligated to help you."

"I don't want him *obligated* to me. If all he did was surf every day and call his mother once a week, I'd still love him and be happy to be around him. I'm glad he's taking over the business, but I don't want to see him miserable because of it. If it takes giving up a little profit to hire help so that he can get out there and surf or spend time with a pretty woman—" he glanced at her "—then he needs to do it."

Gus made it sound simple, however, she knew it was anything but. When you were the person ultimately responsible for a business on which others depended for their livelihood, you couldn't afford to make the wrong decision.

"Are you telling her all my secrets, Grandpa?" Drew, hair and clothes rumpled, shuffled into the room. He gave Sara a secretive smile and brushed his hand across her shoulder as he passed, sending a shiver of pleasure through her.

"Every one," Gus said. "You'll be defenseless."

Drew poured himself a cup of coffee. "Did you save me any pancakes?"

"They're in the oven." Gus checked his watch, a black plastic diver's model that looked straight out of the seventies. "I have to be on the *Sin on the Beach* set in twenty minutes, so I need to get out of here soon."

"How is the filming going?" Sara asked. "Are you enjoying being part of the show?"

"Well…" He rubbed his chin. "You know when they asked me to do it, I had this idea I'd spend the day hanging out with all these gorgeous women, say a few lines and go home. But it's not like that at all."

"It isn't?"

He shook his head. "Nope. All the gorgeous women are hiding in their trailers or busy in makeup while the rest of us bit players sit around on the sand for hours waiting to be called in. And then the director or one of his flunkies tells us to 'Stand there, say this, look over here" and then we do it all over again. Sometimes twenty times."

"That sounds pretty boring."

"I tell you, if the rest of the world were run like a television show, none of us would ever get anything done."

"My friend Ellie is an extra on the show right now," she said. "Maybe you've seen her—she has streaked blond hair, petite, with tattoos."

"The Queen of Evil?" Of course he would remember Ellie's most striking piece of body art, tattooed across her lower back. He grinned. "I've met her. A nice young woman. We talked about coffee."

Sara laughed. "One of Ellie's favorite subjects."

"She and that director fellow, Bill, spend a lot of time making eyes at each other. It's pretty clear—at least to this old dude—that they'd like nothing better than to be alone and naked."

She stifled a gasp, which led him to laugh out loud. "You young people all think you invented sex. Hah!"

"No, we just perfected it." Drew carried a plate of pancakes to the table and sat next to Sara.

"You know what they say, practice makes perfect." Gus winked at Sara. "I guess that applies to sex as well as surfing."

Drew groaned and Gus laughed, then waved goodbye and headed out. When he was gone, Drew set down his fork and turned to Sara. "How are you doing this morning?" he asked, his voice low and sexy.

"I'm doing great." She smiled down at the table, afraid if she looked him in the eyes she'd melt right there on the spot. "It was nice of your grandfather to cook me breakfast."

"As I told you last night, he likes you. He doesn't make his famous flapjacks for just anyone." He sipped more coffee. "What did the two of you talk about before I came down?"

"You, of course." She laughed at the concerned expression on his face. "He thinks you work too hard and you should hire someone to do the books so that you can have more time off," she said.

"Oh he does, does he? And I suppose he thinks if you tell me this, I'll listen."

She shrugged. She wasn't in a position to talk anyone into working less. "I think you should do what you want to do. I'm just reporting our conversation." She carried his plate to the sink. "What are your plans for this morning?"

"I have to be at the shop at ten, but we've got time to catch a few waves before then."

"You want to go surfing?" She'd been sure he'd suggest going back upstairs to bed.

"I can think of a lot of things I'd like to do with you." He gave her a wicked grin. "But if you're going to compete on Saturday, you could use the extra practice."

So, after quick stops at the beach house to retrieve her swimsuit and the Surf Shack to pick up a couple of boards, they hit the water. Drew had her go through all the basic moves again, from paddling out to standing on the board. Three times in a row she fell hard, flipping off her board and floundering in the surf.

"Why am I so awful?" she wailed. "I was much better yesterday."

"You're too far back," Drew said, swimming over to her after her third fall. "You need to stay more forward. Find your balance."

Her fourth try she managed to stay aboard, though she still felt clumsy and ungainly. When she'd ridden out the wave and sunk into the water once more, resting with her elbows propped on her board, Drew swam over to her once more. "That was much better," he said. "You're getting a feel for it."

"I must be crazy to think I can compete after only four days of surfing," she said. She hated not being able to do something well.

"It's the newcomers category. The rules specifically say you have to have been surfing less than a month."

She turned her head to look at him. His hair was slicked back and water ran down the side of his face, the droplets catching in the stubble of his beard. She fought the urge to reach out and flick them away. "Why even bother with a competition for newbies like that?" she asked.

He shrugged. "Official contests wouldn't do it, but the festival organizers wanted to encourage as much participation as possible. They know a lot of people here are fans and they want to play to them. And you're doing it to earn points, right?"

"Yes, and to give myself a reason to work at this beyond I've always wanted to surf.'

"Isn't that a good enough reason?"

"Yes. But I guess it's been so long since I did something solely because it's what I wanted that I had to trick myself a little." One more step in rediscovering her inner wild child. She laughed. "That probably sounds pathetic to you. See why I needed this vacation?"

She looked over her shoulder at the waves rolling toward them. "Should I try again?"

"Let's rest here a little longer."

She turned back to him. They bobbed along side by side in the waves, gradually moving closer to shore. The hot sun caressed her shoulders and the cooler seawater felt good around her legs and hips. "If only I had learned to surf when I was a teenager," she said. "Think how good I'd be now."

"You're still young," Drew said. "You've got plenty of time to get good at it if that's what you want."

"Do you think I could be as good as you?"

He shrugged. "Sure. But I'm not that good. Not like the pros."

"So did you ever think about becoming a pro?"

"I think Grandpa thought I'd follow in his footsteps and be a surfing champion, too, but it didn't work out," he said.

"What happened?"

"Typical teenager, I guess. I was more interested in girls and cars than spending the requisite hours in the water practicing my moves. Then I went off to college and graduated and went to work."

"I still can't believe you were ever an insurance adjuster."

"Yeah." He laughed. "I guess when you grow up living on the beach with parents who run a surf shop, your idea of rebellion is to get a job where you have to wear a suit and tie and work in a cubicle."

She shook her head. "I can't really picture you in a cubicle farm."

"I did all right for a few years. Probably would have kept at it if Grandpa hadn't gotten sick." He rubbed the back of his neck. "I had this idea I was going to work hard, make a lot of money and live the good life."

"Do you ever think about going back to that life?"

"Hell, no! Leaving was the best decision I ever made, though I didn't see it at the time."

"So you really weren't cut out for the work?"

He shook his head. "No. When I came back here and took out my old board, it was as if that tie I'd had to wear had been cutting off my circulation. I couldn't get over how great it felt to be back at the beach. And not just being able to surf again, but doing my own thing in a casual setting. I'm glad I had the business background because it really helped me jump into running the Surf Shack right away. I understand about things like accounting and inventory control. But I'm also glad I didn't have to wait until I was forty and have a midlife crisis to wake up to the fact that that lifestyle really wasn't for me." He glanced at her. "No offense or anything."

She smiled. "It's all right. I don't work in a

cubicle. I have a nice, big office and pretty much make my own schedule." Of course, that usually meant ten- and twelve-hour days, six and seven days a week, but she'd never minded. She thrived on work and if it kept her from having much of a social life, she hadn't really felt the lack.

Until now. Being with Drew reminded her of all she'd been missing out on. Floating beside him in the water now, her every sense was attuned to him—the way the breeze ruffled his hair, the hard curve of muscle across his chest, the smoothness of his skin when he brushed against her. She was hyper-aware of him as a man and of herself as a woman. Could the fact that they'd been all over each other this week have anything to do with her long period of celibacy?

As if reading her mind, he set his board to drift and moved over beside her. "What time is it?" he asked.

"You're the one with the watch."

"Almost time for me to get to work," he said, not bothering to look at the time piece. He put his hand on her stomach, his fingers splayed there, her skin warming at his touch. "I just realized I haven't kissed you this morning."

"Yes, and I've missed it terri—"

His lips covered hers before she had finished speaking. His mouth was warm and firm, his tongue licking salt from her lips, teasing the delicate flesh on the inside of her cheek. She turned and wrapped her legs around his waist, still keeping one arm on her board, the other holding onto him.

They kissed for a long time, a leisurely indulgence. The urgency of desire simmered just below the surface, not demanding or insistent, but present if they decided to let it out.

At last he pulled back. "I really do have to get to work," he said.

"I know." She slipped her legs from around him and claimed her board once more. "See you tonight?"

"Definitely."

They paddled to shore together, then he took the boards and turned one way, while she headed the other. Humming to herself, she was aware of him watching her all the way down the beach.

At the beach house, she was surprised to find Candy getting ready to go out. "Tell me why you're getting dressed up again?" she asked, watching her friend add a blazer to a cocktail dress and panty hose ensemble.

"The Business Women's Awards Luncheon." Candy checked her look in the mirror. "Matt will get to practice networking, and I can talk up my consumer software idea with potential clients. Best of all, we'll get a taste of being back in the work world together."

"Uh-huh."

Just then, Ellie descended the stairs. "What's happening?" she asked.

"Candy's going to a business luncheon with Matt," Sara said. "Welcome to Bizarro World. Candy's working all the time and all I can think of is playing with Drew." She couldn't hold back a smile. She'd actually tried to piece together her usual to-do list on the walk from the Surf Shack, but Be with Drew had ended up on every line. She fantasized about spending whole days—and nights—with him, playing in the surf, sunning on the beach, making love for hours, with no responsibilities or obligations pulling at them.

Lost in such happy daydreams, Sara missed most of whatever Ellie was saying. "Everything worked out," was all she caught. What was working out well? Definitely she and Drew, but she hadn't said anything to Ellie and Candy about that. Maybe Ellie meant Candy and Matt. Or maybe even Ellie and Bill. Gus did say they'd looked pretty cozy on the set….

But Ellie had already moved on to the idea of Candy starting her own business. "Don't you want your own agency anyway?" Ellie asked.

"In five years, sure," Candy said. "When I have enough experience. I'm not leaving SynchUp yet. That would be way too flaky."

"Starting your own agency is not flaky," Sara said. "You'd be your own boss, depending on yourself for your income. You'd love that, Candy. I think you'd shine." Of course, she herself wouldn't be able to do such a thing. Not with Uncle Spence to consider. But Candy had no such ties.

Ellie and Candy debated the topic a bit longer. Sara moved to her computer. She really should think about getting some work done. She probably had a hundred e-mails to answer.

When the computer was up and running, the icon

for the spreadsheet she'd created for the festival caught her eye. "Let's see where we stand on points before you leave," she said. In addition to logging their points, she'd inputted the information they'd been able to learn about other teams. The three women studied the chart on the computer. "Our biggest competition is that team from Santa Monica—those cheaters," she said. "We have to outwit them somehow."

"If you win the surfing competition, that'd be great," Candy said.

She nodded. That was a big *if*. "I'm going to find a few more ways to earn points," she said. "If we all do that, it will help a lot."

Then Matt arrived and they were saying goodbye to Candy. "The two of them look good together, don't you think?" Ellie asked, waving as her brother and Candy drove away.

"They do," Sara agreed. She still couldn't get over this odd role reversal. Usually, she was the one rushing off to a business meeting while Ellie and Candy tried to talk her into taking it easy.

She glanced at Ellie, who was gazing toward the ocean, a dreamy look on her face. "How are things going with you and Bill?" she asked.

"Great. No, amazing."

Sara grinned. Ellie was definitely over the moon for this Bill guy. Sara wanted to find out more, but her phone rang. Hoping it was Drew, she rushed to answer it, only to be greeted by Uncle Spence's voice. "Sara, you've got to help me," he said.

She rolled her eyes. "What is it this time, Uncle Spence?" Whatever it was, she would handle it. She always did. As much as she enjoyed the fantasy of spending her days as a surfer girl, the reality was that the life would probably bore her to death after a few days. Like Drew, she took her responsibilities seriously. There were times when work *had* to come first. Thank God he understood that.

AFTER LEAVING Sara, Drew had a hard time focusing on work. Instead of considering board wax and rash guards, he found himself remembering the way she'd felt in his arms, or the funny flutter he got in his chest whenever she smiled at him.

Having her in his life made him look at everything differently. He'd resisted the idea of hiring another employee before. After all, his parents were counting on him to take care of the family business personally. But if Gus didn't really mind, why not think about hiring someone to help him? Especially if doing so meant he'd have more time to spend with Sara.

Yes, she was due to leave Malibu in a few days, but it wasn't as though L.A. was so far away. And she obviously loved it here on the beach. She could spend weekends here, and he could make the occasional trip into the city. They'd find a way to work things out....

A man with a very shiny, very pink bald head came into the shop, pulling Drew out of his daydream. He tried not to stare at the man's shiny dome and white, white skin, and focused instead on the bright-red-and-yellow Hawaiian shirt he wore. "Hello. Can I help you?" he asked.

The man removed his sunglasses and fixed Drew with a look that left him a little disoriented. It was the kind of look his old boss at the insurance company liked to give him when the figures on a repair estimate didn't add up to the number the boss wanted—as if Drew was personally responsible for the discrepancy. "I could ask you the same question," the man said after a moment. "But since I'm off duty, I won't." He turned away and began examining a display of T-shirts.

Drew frowned. Was the guy nuts? Something about him was familiar, but he couldn't say what. "Are you looking for something in particular?" he asked.

"I need sunscreen," the man said. "I'm out." He turned to face Drew again, grinning this time. "Got anything I can put on this dome?"

"Old-fashioned zinc oxide's a good bet." Drew walked over to a display of the traditional lifeguard's favorite. "It comes in colors now. You can paint it on like warpaint." He pointed to another shelf. "We also have some pretty good sports block. SPF 45. Of course, nothing works forever in the water. You have to keep applying it. More often if your skin is more sensitive."

"Yes, you could say I'm sensitive." The man chose a tube of the sport block and took it to the front counter.

Drew rang up the sale, trying to ignore the hinky vibe he was getting from the guy. Was the guy casing the place for a robbery or something?

"How's it going with your girl?" the man asked as he collected his change.

"My girl?" Drew frowned at him. What was this guy getting at?

"The one you were with at the carnival. Sara."

How did he know about Sara? Drew's hands curled into fists. "Dude, do I know you?"

The man smiled again. "Not as well as I know you, obviously." He struck a pose. "Picture me in a turban."

Then it hit him. That first night with Sara at the carnival. *Truth or Bare.* "Magellan!" He stared at the carnival showman.

The man nodded. "Amazing what a great disguise a turban can be."

"Yeah." He hadn't really thought of the carnival performers as having lives outside of the midway. He searched for something else to say. "Do you surf?"

"No, I just came in for sunblock." He tucked the tube into his pocket. "So how is Sara?"

"Sara is fine."

Magellan shook his head. "Fine-looking, yes. Doing fine? Maybe not as well as she thinks. She still has a little problem with her uncle. Or maybe the problem is more with Sara herself."

This implied criticism of Sara set Drew's teeth on edge. This crackpot didn't even know her. "There's nothing wrong with Sara," he said.

"No need to get angry with me." Magellan held up his hands. "After all, you've still got your own problems to work through."

"My biggest problem right now is you spouting off about things you don't know anything about."

Magellan nodded. "I get that a lot. People don't like to hear the truth." He waved, then turned and walked out.

Drew stared after him. The other night he'd been impressed by Magellan's psychic abilities. But then Drew had been intoxicated with his newfound attraction to Sara, which led him to see everything in a positive light.

Now, without the bright lights and costuming, the loud music and crowds and carnival atmosphere, Magellan struck Drew as an arrogant poser.

A poser who didn't know anything about him, or about Sara. Sure, her uncle was a little demanding, but Sara knew how to handle him. This vacation had shown her how important it was to make time for herself.

The two of them were on the same wave-length. They were perfect for each other.

AFTER Sara had solved Uncle Spence's crisis du jour, and helped him script exactly what he would say to a new client at a closing that afternoon, she studied the spreadsheet she'd made of their contest points. Candy and Ellie were doing their share to earn points but she was woefully behind. She grabbed up the flyer and studied it again. Freak dancing, body painting, a Good Vibrations contest, couples sand sculpture, I Scream You Scream ice cream sundae contest… But what would she be good at?

Better yet, what could she do that Drew could

help her with? Not that she needed an excuse to see him again, but she liked the idea of an activity they could both be involved in. She wanted to spend as much time with him as possible and since the festival wasn't awarding points for having sex—at least not actual sex—she'd settle for something that would allow them to be together and contribute points to their team.

"You still at that computer?" Ellie appeared in the doorway. "Shut that thing off and go play," she said.

"I will." Sara shut the computer. "I was just looking at the spreadsheet for the contest. We need more points."

"We'll get them. There are lots of activities going on all week. Could I borrow that pinky-brown eyeshadow you used on me earlier in the week?"

"Sure." She stood and fetched her makeup bag from the bathroom adjoining her room. "So the makeover is growing on you?" she asked as she dug through the various bottles and compacts of makeup. The new hair color really suited Ellie's complexion, and the softer cosmetic colors made her look sexier and more sophisticated.

"I haven't decided." Ellie fluffed her hair. "I'm still working on making it my own. I don't want to lose the goth thing altogether. Maybe instead of glam goth I'll go with Bohemian goth. Or beach goth."

Sara laughed and handed over the eyeshadow. "Beach goth?"

"You know—black string bikini, maybe a dog collar and cuffs, dramatic makeup. It could work."

"I believe you could make it work."

"Hey, give me a little warpaint and I'll be turning heads in no time." She waved the little compact of eye shadow.

Paint. "That's it," Sara said. She grabbed up the flyer again. "I'll enter the body-painting competition. It's this afternoon, on the beach. It's sponsored by some zinc sunblock maker."

Ellie grinned. "Will you be the painter—or the canvas?"

"I think I'll let Drew be the artist." The idea of his hands on her—all over her—sent a pleasant thrill through her. "I don't think he'll object to the idea, do you?"

"I doubt many men would." Ellie studied the flyer. "Bill and I are entering the Good Vibrations contest tonight."

Ellie's words were casual, but her voice had a dreamy quality and her smile was that of a woman who was picturing a man she lusted after—naked. Sara nudged her. "So things are going well for you?" she asked.

Ellie's grin broadened. "Things are…going."

They laughed. Sara hugged her. "Thanks for making me take this vacation," she said. "It's been fantastic."

"Even with all Uncle Spence's interruptions?"

"They haven't been that bad. And I've been able to handle him and have a great time." If nothing else, the week had proved to her she *could* juggle work and a relationship. It was all about prioritizing what was the most important at the moment. Fortunately, Drew understood that, too.

"And meet a really hot guy," Ellie said.

"That, too. A really hot guy." One who warmed more than her body. She'd really hit the jackpot with Drew. He was the perfect man for her.

9

WHEN Sara called Drew, he seemed only too happy to turn the Surf Shack over to Cooter for the afternoon and meet her at the beach. "I think this is going to give me a whole new appreciation for zinc sunblock," he said, eyeing the eight-pack of zinc crayons they'd been issued.

"We need to come up with a good idea of what to paint," she said. She'd worn her tiniest blue bikini, but was beginning to feel a little nervous about having her body on display for so many people.

"I have a few ideas, don't worry," he said, in a sexy growl that sent a shiver through her.

"Remember folks, anything goes, so be creative," the announcer instructed. "You have one hour to complete your masterpieces, starting now!"

Around them, the other contestants cheered and ripped open the containers. Drew stepped back and studied Sara. "What are you thinking of painting?" she asked.

He reached into his pocket and pulled out something and handed it to her. "Go to the ladies' room and put these on. I'll meet you over there."

She looked at the objects in her hand. "Band-Aids?" Tiny ones at that—the round spots her mom used to put over ant bites so she wouldn't scratch them.

"Take off your top and put them on over your nipples, then let me in when I knock on the door." He put his hands on her shoulder and turned her toward the restrooms across the way. "Go on. We don't have much time."

Curious, and a little turned on by the idea, she hurried to the ladies' room, locked the door, and peeled off her top. The bandages barely covered her nipples. She studied her reflection in the mirror. Her breasts were white against her tan, paler even than the beige bandages.

There was a hard knock on the door. "It's me," Drew said. "Let me in before someone sees me."

She opened the door and he slipped inside and quickly locked it after him, then turned to her. His expression immediately heated. "You look amazing," he said. He pulled her to him and kissed her, his body pressed against hers, his erection hard against her stomach.

She arched against him, tempted to blow off the contest entirely and have sex right here up against the bathroom door.

But he possessed a little more self control. He gently pushed her away and handed her a small tub of blue paste. "Take this and rub it all over your breasts. Pretend you're drawing on a bikini top. One of those with no straps that just wraps around."

"A bandeau." She looked at the blue paste. "This isn't the stuff they gave us to use."

"It's the same stuff, but it's from my shop. Easier to cover a large area with than the crayon."

She looked skeptical. "Is that cheating?"

"I listened and nowhere in the rules did the announcer say we were limited to what they gave us. It's still zinc oxide, so I figure we're safe."

"Let me get this straight. I'm going to go out there on the beach wearing only two Band-Aids and paint?"

"And your bikini bottoms. Now hurry up and smear it on."

"It's a crazy idea," she said, even as she began rubbing the blue paste across her chest.

"It's not like you'll really be topless," he said. "I mean, once I get done, no one will even know unless they look really close."

"If you say so." She scooped up more paste. "This stuff is thick and hard to work with."

"I'll help," he said. "Otherwise it will take all day."

He began applying the sunblock, using his fingers to spread it liberally over her skin. She'd been getting turned on rubbing her own breasts but when he touched her the effect was an immediate jolt of heat straight to her groin. As he stroked and rubbed, she squirmed and fought the urge to moan.

"Stand still," he said. "I'm trying to get this even."

"It's hard to stand still when you're touching me like this."

He looked up and met her gaze, and she saw her own

arousal reflected there. "Like this?" he said, and deliberately dragged his thumb across her bandaged nipple.

"Yes," she gasped, and reached to pull him closer.

"We have to do this right if we want to win the contest," he said, pretending to ignore the move. But his strokes became more deliberate, circling her nipple, then rubbing it, until she had to hold onto the sink to stay upright.

He stepped back and studied his work, then nodded to the mirror. "Take a look," he said.

She turned and was surprised at what she saw. The blue swath of paint did look very much like a bandeau top, the thickness of the paste effectively hiding the bandages. He had left a deep sweep of cleavage bare, as well as the underside of each breast. He traced these bare patches now with his fingers, his erection pressed firmly to her backside. "Very sexy," he said, and kissed her neck.

She leaned back, grinding against him, wishing surfers favored Speedos. She imagined what he'd look like with the head of his penis peeking out over the waistband of a scrap of Lycra, his balls and the rest of his shaft outlined clearly against the tight fabric.

He moved his hands to her ass and began stroking her. "Do you mind if this suit gets paint on it?" he asked. "I can't guarantee it will come out."

"It's for a good cause," she said. Though what she really wanted was to take the swimsuit bottom off, along with his board shorts.

He turned her around to face him once more. "We'd better get busy. You just stand still while I work."

"What are you painting?" she asked, as he opened several jars and crayons and arranged them on the ledge of the sink.

"You'll see," he said. "I just hope I'm good enough to pull it off."

"Have you painted before?" she asked, trying to ignore the quivering in her thighs when he began to cover them with more blue paint.

"I took an oils class in college. I needed an elective and thought it might be fun." He grinned. "I wanted to take nude drawing, but that class was filled. Anyway, I was better at it than I expected, but it's been awhile."

He was rubbing paint on the inside of her thighs now, and she surrendered to the growing arousal within her. This was probably the most unusual foreplay she'd ever participated in, but definitely among the most enjoyable.

The sound of laughter nearby distracted her. "I think someone's out there," she whispered.

Drew froze, and they both stared at the door. Sure enough, the doorknob rattled and someone knocked.

Sara looked at Drew and shook her head. If she said the room was occupied, the person or persons on the other side would just wait. If she kept quiet, maybe the person would go away.

Drew motioned her into the stall. "Sit down and pull your feet up so you can't be seen," he whispered. "I'm going to get rid of them."

Stifling laughter at the absurdity of the situation, she did as he asked, watching through the crack between the stall door and the frame as he opened the door and stuck his head out. "Sorry, ladies," he said. "This one's out of order."

"What are you doing in the ladies' room?" A high-pitched voice demanded.

"I'm the plumber. I'm trying to get the toilet unstopped. Things are a mess in here." He leaned farther out the door, pointing. "There's another restroom about a quarter mile down the beach."

"Ewww!" Without further argument, the women left.

Drew closed the door and turned to Sara. "You can come out now," he said.

"A plumber?" she laughed. "Since when do plumbers wear board shorts and T-shirts?"

"Hey, I'm a Malibu plumber." He tore off a sheet of paper towel, grabbed one of the zinc sticks and wrote Out of Order in large letters. Another glob of zinc on the back served as glue to stick the sign to the door. "That should keep us from being interrupted again," he said.

He turned back to her, grinning. "Now where were we?"

"You were turning me into the blue woman."

"Oh yeah."

He knelt before her and reached for a second tub of blue sunblock. He covered her stomach to just below her navel, and all her legs, then turned her around to coat her hips and bottom. Finally, he covered the front of her bikini bottom with the thick blue paste, working quickly, not lingering over her crotch, though she made several thrusts forward, encouraging him.

"Wait, we're not even to the best part yet," he said. "How much time do we have left?"

While he finished painting the tops of her feet she pulled her cell phone from her bag and checked the time. "We have about thirty minutes left."

"Great. Is your phone switched off?"

"No, but it's okay. This is Uncle Spence's afternoon at his gym. He won't call me during his workout."

"Is that all he does—play golf, go to dinner and the gym?"

"He spends a lot of time in the office, just not as much now that I'm there. He worked hard by himself for a lot of years, so I guess he figures he deserves to take time off now."

He nodded. "I guess so." He pulled out one of the green crayons and began making sweeping strokes down her legs.

"Was Gus still on the *Sin on the Beach* set when you left the Surf Shack?" she asked.

"I guess so." He stroked green paint up the inside of her leg and across her mons, making her gasp.

"You like that?" he asked, grinning.

"Mmm." She shifted her weight to her other leg, wondering how long she could bear to stand here this way, thinking of all the things she wished he would do to her.

He switched to black paint, using more sweeping strokes, blending with his thumbs, so intent on his work she wondered if he was even aware of her as more than a canvas for his art.

When the black, green and blue paints were blended to his liking, he reached for the white. He applied this in swirls and sweeps, up her thighs and across her abdomen, curling around her navel. "What are you doing?" she asked. From this angle, the painting looked entirely abstract.

"You'll see." He added more dabs of white, and rocked back on his heels to study the effect. "Turn around and look in the mirror," he said.

She turned and was amazed at what she saw. "It looks like I'm standing in the ocean," she said. The swirls of blue, green, black and white looked like churning waves.

"You're Venus rising from the sea," he said. He began to add green, black and white to her backside. "What do you think?"

"It's gorgeous." Simple, but effective.

"Don't forget sexy." He nudged her legs farther apart and applied paint between her legs. "If the judges look close enough to realize you're naked from the waist up, I'd say we're a shoo-in."

"Because we're so daring?" she asked.

"Because you're so beautiful. Hand me a damp paper towel."

She did as he asked and he cleaned his hands. She was about to turn around when his hands on her hips stopped her. "Hold on a minute. I see something here I have to fix."

He rubbed at the paint along the cleavage between

her buttocks, dragging his finger down between her legs and around to the front, over her mons, where he lingered, applying pressure. "How does that feel?" he asked, watching her in the mirror.

"It feels…good." She rocked toward him, wanting more.

"Turn around."

She did so, and he looked up at her. "I don't want to mess up my artwork," he said.

"You can redo it." She didn't care about the artwork right now. She needed him to touch her.

"Maybe we can manage." He slid one finger beneath the edge of her swimsuit bottom, pushing the fabric aside to reveal her sex. The light-brown curls and pink skin stood out against the dark paint, as if in a spotlight.

"I'm afraid my fingers might still have sunblock on them," he said.

"Then wash them."

"No, I have a better idea."

Before she could ask what that idea might be, he leaned forward and swept his tongue across her. The satin heat of him made her knees buckle, and she gripped the edge of the sink once more.

He traced his tongue around the rim of her opening, then plunged it into her, awakening nerve endings she hadn't even known existed. Then he moved back to her clit, stroking it, sucking on it, while she closed her eyes and panted, the wanting within her building.

She could feel the cool porcelain of the sink

against her back, was dimly aware of faint shouts and the bass throb of music from the beach, those sounds almost overwhelmed by the pounding of her own heart and her ragged breathing.

Drew shifted and braced his hands against the sink alongside hers. He plunged his tongue into her once more, and she ached to feel his cock inside her. She opened her mouth to tell him so, but a fresh wave of desire stole her speech as he moved his attentions to her clit once more.

She came clinging to the sink, her thighs trembling, biting her lip to muffle her cries. Her climax rocked her, leaving her shaking, but wanting still more. She looked down at him, kneeling there before her, his mouth wet with her juices. "I want you in me," she said.

"We'll mess up the paint job."

"I don't care about the paint." She reached for him. "I want you."

He rose. "Turn around again."

"What?"

"Turn around. Bend over and brace your hands on the sink."

Seeing what he was getting at, she smiled and turned around. Bent over, she spread her legs, and let out a groan of pleasure when his fingers pulled aside her bikini bottoms once more. She heard the rustle of his board shorts dropping to the floor, and the whisper of a foil packet being torn, then he was standing behind her, entering her from behind.

She bent over more, tilting her pelvis, allowing him

easier access. Each stroke from this angle sent a rush of intense feeling through her. One hand still clutching the sink, she reached down to fondle herself.

He groaned as her muscles tightened around his shaft and his strokes grew harder, faster, until he was slamming into her and she was forced to grip the sink again with both hands. All the delayed gratification of the previous forty-five minutes was unleashed in each stroke, all the waiting and longing crystalized into an intense need translated into intense physicality. It was wild, fierce sex and she reveled in it, biting her lip to keep from screaming out his name as yet another climax shook her.

He clutched her shoulders and drove deeper into her, and she watched in the mirror as passion transformed his face into something more wild and beautiful. He came with an animal growl and she clenched her muscles tightly, wanting to give him as much pleasure as possible.

When he parted from her at last, he was breathing hard, drenched with sweat. "That was incredible," she said, wanting to hug him, but settling instead for leaning forward and kissing him on the mouth.

The kiss was long and deep, the perfect finale to a perfect moment. When they finally broke apart, they both smiled, then he motioned her to turn around once more. "I need to check the paint."

After a couple of touch-ups, he pronounced her ready to go. "What time is it?" he asked.

She checked her cell phone again. "We have five minutes."

"Perfect." He looked her in the eye. "Are you sure you're okay with this?"

She nodded. With all the sunblock coverage, she didn't feel as naked as she'd thought she would. And Drew would be there with her. With him by her side, she could get through anything.

THE SUNLIGHT on the beach was blinding after the dimness in the ladies' room. Drew adjusted his sunglasses and waited for Sara to emerge. He was still a little dazed after their erotic encounter.

He'd been turned on from the moment he came up with the idea of painting her topless. Then the act of painting her had been amazingly sensual. Under the guise of applying the colored sunblock, he'd explored practically every inch of her body, memorizing the feel of the curve of her buttocks, the silken skin behind her knees, and the graceful turn of her ankle. He'd seen her in a way he'd never seen her before—not just as a pretty woman he enjoyed looking at, but as a sensual being who delighted him with the feel of her skin, the scent of her hair and the sound of her sighs.

"Okay, let's go." She appeared behind him. She'd fluffed out her hair until it fell in a wild tangle around her shoulders, adding to her goddess-emerging-from-the-sea look.

"You look great," he said. He kissed her cheek, then took her hand and they walked together across the sand.

"Where have you two been?" One of the members

of the Santa Monica team asked when Drew and Sara took their place in the row of contestants.

"I had to go to the ladies' room," Sara said, then turned her back on him.

"Dude, she's not wearing any top," another member of the team said.

Sara's cheeks flushed, but Drew was impressed that she kept her cool. "Of course I am," she said. "Don't be ridiculous."

"I tell you she's not." The guy reached out as if to grab Sara's breast, but Drew put out a hand to stop him. "I wouldn't do that if I were you," he said. Not that he considered himself a tough guy, but he wouldn't hesitate to land a solid punch or two in defense of Sara.

"Dudes and dudettes, time to start the judging," the announcer interrupted them. "Take your places, strike a pose, whatever. Let's get started."

A reggae beat blared from the speakers and the spectators hooted and applauded as one of the supporting players from *Sin On the Beach,* accompanied by the sunblock manufacturer's representative and a local tanning salon owner, studied the line of contestants.

While the judges made notes and conferred among themselves, Drew studied the competition. The Santa Monica team had gone with a graffiti girl theme, with the female member of their team liberally covered with words and sayings rendered in bright colors, including a flagrant plug for the manufacturer in bright blue down one leg. She danced to the music and blew kisses to the crowd as she waited for the judges to approach.

Another group had painted one of their women as a mermaid, complete with a shell bra and a green sarong for the tail. They'd get points for creativity, he decided, but they hadn't in fact used all that much product.

One woman was covered with colored polka dots. The effect was of an unfortunate rash. One was candy-striped in pink and white. Maybe she was a candy cane? Or a county jail inmate?

"Maybe the topless thing is more obvious than we thought." Sara leaned close to whisper to him. "You don't think they'll arrest us or anything do you?"

He shook his head. "You're cool. I promise the judges will love it. After all, you're not actually naked. It's just the *idea* that's exciting."

"It got you pretty excited, didn't it?" she teased.

"And you." He rubbed his hand lightly along her backside. Already he couldn't wait to get her alone again.

The judges reached her and the actor lowered his sunglasses and gave her a long look. "You're practically naked under that paint, aren't you?" he asked.

"Only to prove this sunblock protects even the tenderest parts," she said with a smile.

The sunblock rep seemed to like that idea. He smiled and nodded and wrote something on his clipboard.

"Did you do the painting?" the tanning parlor owner asked Drew.

"Yeah. I was going for Venus rising from the waves."

"Interesting," the man said.

The judges moved on. Sara leaned close again. "What do you think?"

"The sunblock rep and the actor were definitely impressed. The tanning parlor owner is harder to read."

The judges were with the Santa Monica team now, and the woman with them was pointing out some of the graffiti written on her legs and back. "She's really cute," Sara said.

"Yeah, but how much creativity does it take to write words on someone?"

"Creativity is only twenty percent of the scoring."

"Yeah, but use of the product is forty percent. We used more product that almost anyone. Except maybe the candy striper."

The judges moved off a little ways to confer. Sara shifted from one foot to the other. "I wish they'd hurry," she said. "It's hot out here and my skin's starting to itch."

"It washes off in the surf. We can go for a swim as soon as they give us our trophy."

"You're really confident we're going to win, aren't you?"

"You're the hottest-looking woman here and with three male judges I'm betting that's what it comes down to."

The look she gave him could have melted ice. "You don't think you're a little bit prejudiced?"

"I'm only telling the truth." He grinned.

"All right folks, looks like we have a winner."

The announcer silenced the crowd. "First, let's get our three finalists up front here. Couples number six, nine and two, step forward please."

"That's us!" Sara squealed and clapped, and she and Drew joined the mermaid and graffiti girl next to the judges.

"The judges have cast their votes, but the crowd also gets to participate," the announcer said. "Let's see if you agree with the judges. Signal your favorite when I point. First we have, from team number nine, Bill's Beach Bums, a Malibu mermaid."

Whistles and cheers greeted the mermaid, who smiled and waved at her fans.

"Next, team number two, the Santa Monica Marvels, brings us Graffiti Grrl."

The woman in question did a few dance steps and waved while the crowd signaled its approval.

"Last, but not least, from team number six, the Java Mamas, we have a naughty Venus. Look close, folks, and tell me what's *not* there." This comment brought another blush from Sara, and a wildly enthusiastic response from the crowd.

The announcer grinned and a drumroll began to play. "Looks like the crowd agrees with the judges. Ladies and gentleman, for five hundred points and this lovely trophy, the winner is our naughty Venus!"

Drew whooped and pulled Sara into his arms, being careful not to smear her paint. They accepted their trophy and points voucher, then posed for pictures—by themselves, with the judges, with the announcer, with the actor alone. Several spectators also took pictures. "Righteous paint job, dude," one man said, giving a two-thumbs-up sign.

"Can we leave now?" Sara asked when the last camera clicked. "This sunblock is drying out and starting to crack. And I think one of my Band-Aids is loose."

The prospect of an impromptu unveiling was interesting, but not something Drew wanted to happen in public. "Let's go down the beach to where it's not so crowded," Drew said. "You go in the water and I'll grab your swimsuit top and bring it to you."

While she waded out and ducked down in the water, he retrieved her swimsuit top from her bag and walked out to meet her. "Thanks," she said, reaching for the top.

"Not yet." He held the top out of her reach. "I don't think you've gotten all the sunblock off." He reached out and rubbed at a spot of blue and green, then another of black.

She reached for the top again. "Wait, there's a few more."

"You're not rubbing off sunblock now," she said, her voice a little breathless.

"Maybe not." He pulled her close, excited at the prospect of having sex right here in the ocean again.

"Is that Gus over there?"

The mention of his grandfather stopped his libido in its tracks. "Where?"

"On that surfboard." She bounced up, shielding her eyes with one hand, and indicated a surfer riding a set of waves farther down the shore.

Drew stared at the familiar white-haired figure with the pot belly and the bright-red board shorts. "Gus!" he shouted, but the waves swallowed up his voice.

Fear grabbed hold of Drew's heart and squeezed. "He's not supposed to be surfing," he said. "It's too strenuous. What if he has another heart attack?"

"It'll be okay." Sara clutched his arm. "He looks fine. And it's not a big wave."

"He promised me he wouldn't do this." He turned toward the beach. "I have to go talk to him," he said, thrusting her swimsuit top into her hand.

"Do you want me to come with you?" she asked.

He shook his head. "No, I need to talk to him alone." This time, he needed to make his grandfather understand how important it was not to take risks like this.

"Will I see you at the party tonight?" she asked.

He'd almost forgotten about the big beach party. "If Grandpa's feeling okay, I'll be there," he said. "If not, I'll call you."

She splashed toward him and kissed him hard on the cheek. "It'll be okay," she whispered.

He wanted to believe her, but he'd seen Gus after his second heart attack when he'd looked anything but okay. That experience had taught Drew there was no taking chances with your health and doctor's orders. Not when you were seventy years old.

Not when you were talking about the only grandfather he had.

10

By the time Drew caught up with his grandfather, Gus was surrounded by half a dozen young men and women who were peppering him with questions and hanging on his every word. Drew resisted the urge to roll his eyes. What was it with his grandpa and his groupies?

Gus stood in the middle of his circle of admirers, surfboard propped at his side, chest puffed out, grinning from ear to ear. But Drew could see he was breathing hard, and his face looked pale beneath his tan. If nothing else, he must be worn out from the strain of holding his stomach in so long.

Drew waded into the crowd and took hold of Gus's arm. "Sorry, folks, I need this guy back at the shop," he said.

Everyone made appropriate sounds of disappointment. A babe in a red bikini clutched at Gus's other arm. "I'll see you tonight at the party, won't I, Gus?" she asked.

"Of course I'll be there, Dierdre," Gus said. "I wouldn't miss it."

"Come on, *Grandpa*," Drew tucked the surfboard under his arm and tugged Gus away.

When they were clear of the crowd, Gus jerked his arm out of Drew's grasp. "What's the big idea?" he said. "Are you jealous?"

"Are you *crazy?*" Drew turned to glare at him. "What do you think you were doing out there?"

"Just showing the guys and gals from the set a few moves." He stroked his moustache. "They've been after me all week to put on a demonstration."

"Which you had no business doing. Do you want to risk another heart attack?"

Gus dismissed the idea with a shake of his head. "I could surf little waves like that in my sleep."

"Then how come you were out of breath?"

"You're imagining things. I'm in terrific shape."

"Maybe for a man who's seventy who's had two heart attacks." He stopped and faced his grandfather. "I almost had a heart attack myself when I saw you out there. Promise me you won't take chances like that again."

Gus looked away. "I've been surfing since I was fifteen years old. I always said I'd do it until the day I died."

Drew's throat tightened. "I want that day to be a long time in the future."

Gus shook his head. "I already promised the festival organizers that I'd give a demonstration before the surfing competition on Saturday."

"What about your promise to me? You said if I got out and participated in the festival, you'd behave yourself and take it easy."

Gus looked at him at last, his expression surprisingly tender. "You worry too much," he said. "Nothing's going to happen to me. I feel great."

"You feel great now. I want you to stay that way. And I have reason to worry. You can't pretend those two heart attacks didn't happen."

"Your worrying doesn't change anything about the past or the future," Gus said. "Life is like surfing—the key is balance. If you lean too far one way or the other, you're going to fall off."

Drew frowned. He hated when Gus assumed the role of the grand philosopher. "What the hell is that supposed to mean?" he asked.

"It means that if I have to spend the rest of my life on shore, not doing something I love, I'm leaning too far toward safety and I'm going to be miserable." He patted Drew's arm. "I have to live my life. I may not do things how you like them, but I know you love me anyway." Smiling, he took the surfboard from Drew and made his way toward the Surf Shack.

Drew stared after him, fists knotted in frustration. He did love Gus. More than almost anyone else in his life. The second heart attack had frightened them all badly, reminding them that even though Gus acted young, he wasn't a kid anymore. Another heart attack could mean the end of him. The thought of losing him made Drew's chest hurt. He didn't want to interfere with Gus's enjoyment of life, but he wanted to be sure there was still as much as possible of that life left. Why couldn't Gus see that? Why did he have to be so stubborn?

SARA WENT all out for the party that evening, trading in shorts and swimsuits for a beaded mini dress she'd snagged from a boutique near the Surf Shack. While she was getting ready, Candy came in, looking dazed, and announced that she and Matt were officially "in love."

The words made goose pimples rise on Sara's arms. *Love.* Such a wonderful, powerful, dangerous word. Though she and Drew had danced around the idea themselves, she hadn't found the courage to actually say the words out loud. Was it really possible to love someone after only a few days? Her practical nature told her she should wait until they'd known each other longer, see how things went once she was back in L.A. in her real world. How much of her feelings for Drew were due to the intoxication of a summer fling and rediscovering the wild woman inside her and how much was the real thing?

She heard the music from the festivities and saw the smoke from the bonfires long before she reached the site. One end of the beach had been transformed into party central, complete with several busy bars, dancing and more games and competitions to earn points. She and Drew should sign up for something—freak dancing, maybe?

She grinned at the idea of rubbing her body provocatively against his to an erotic, driving beat. She couldn't be around the man five minutes without getting turned on. On the dance floor they might very well explode!

She realized finding Drew in the crowd might be

a challenge. She stood on tiptoe and scanned the mass of revelers. She spotted Candy and Matt, their attention focused on each other. The knowledge that her friend was really and truly in love with a great guy made her smile.

Sara's purse began to vibrate, startling her, until she realized it was her phone, the ring-tone inaudible over the loud music blaring from speakers nearby. Her hand over one ear, she dug out her phone, hoping it wasn't Drew calling to cancel.

"Sara! You've got to come home this instant." Uncle Spence's voice came through loud and clear.

"What is it? What's wrong?" she asked, alarmed. "Is Mom okay?"

"Your mother? Of course she's fine. Why wouldn't she be fine?"

"Then what is so important I need to come home right away?"

"The business is falling apart without you here," he said. "Customers are calling and I can't be expected to keep up with everything myself." His voice rose as he worked himself into a frenzy once more.

"Calm down," she said. "What specifically do you need? I'm sure I can help you over the phone."

"What I need is you here. Haven't you had enough of the beach?"

"It's only been four days." Four of the most wonderful days of her life. And she had two more before she had to leave. She intended to take advantage of every minute.

"Four days is a long time in the business world."

She heard the clink of ice and pictured Spence at his desk, his ever-present glass of iced tea at his side—probably spiked with Jack Daniel's at this hour. "I need you here to talk to these people," he said.

"What people?"

"Your customers. These corporate types expect a lot of coddling. And you know I expect you to give it to them."

"If you don't want to talk to them, put them off," she said. "I'll be back next week and I'll call them then."

"I won't do that," he said, his voice stern. "If we upset them, they might take their business elsewhere."

"I don't think they'll do that," she said. Well, some of them might. But those were the ones she'd just as soon not deal with again anyway. "Be nice and reassure them that everything is being taken care of—there's nothing for them to worry about. You're good at reassuring people that way. I've heard you do it before."

The ice rattled again. "Just come home. I need you."

She spotted a familiar figure moving toward her. Her heart fluttered wildly at the sight of Drew in a bright Hawaiian shirt and chinos. "We'll talk about this later, Uncle Spence," she said. "I have to go now." Then she shoved the phone back into her bag, determined to ignore it if it rang again.

"There you are." Drew grinned and leaned down to kiss her. He smelled good—like lime-tinged aftershave and herbal shampoo. She buried her nose in his neck and inhaled deeply, instantly reminded of last night, lying in his arms.

He drew back and looked her up and down. "Nice dress," he said. "Makes me want to take it off."

She laughed. "We should probably stay at the party at least a little while."

"You're right." He turned to look around them. "And I could use a drink."

"Sounds good." At the nearest bar, they ordered margaritas. While they waited for their drinks, Sara asked, "How's Gus?"

Drew's expression darkened. "Physically, he's fine. For now. Mentally, he obviously has a screw loose."

"What happened this afternoon?" she asked.

"He was showing off for some people from the TV show." He shook his head. "He still likes to impress the women."

Sara laughed and accepted the drink he handed her. "He does have a certain charm." She winked at him. "It runs in the family."

"Yeah, well, apparently common sense doesn't run in the family. He's determined to surf again on Saturday before the competition." He took a long drink. "The festival people asked him to do a demo and I guess his ego wouldn't let him say no."

"It'll be okay," she said. "I'm sure he wouldn't do it if he felt bad."

Drew shook his head. "You don't know how stubborn he can be." He looked around. "But hey, I didn't come here to talk about him. Let's have a good time."

They started walking, squeezing around groups of

dancers, past a lavish buffet complete with carved-ice sculptures and elaborate arrangements of fruit. A barker tried to recruit players for the sexual trivia game, while another hawked the opportunity to compete in a dance contest.

"What's this?" Drew asked. "More contests?"

"It's all about getting points for the competition," Sara said.

"Your team ought to be in pretty good shape after the body-painting contest this afternoon," he said.

She nodded. "I think so. But we don't know what the other teams have been up to. Particularly the Santa Monica team. They were awfully close to us in points."

He finished his drink and tossed the plastic glass into a nearby trash container. "So let's earn some more points." He glanced at the two barkers. "Trivia or dancing?"

"I've never been good at trivia games." She tossed her own empty glass.

"Then that leaves dancing." He grabbed her hand. "Let's go before I change my mind."

When they approached the sign-up table near the dance floor Sara was surprised to see the turbaned psychic from Truth or Bare. "You're Magellan," she said.

"The one and only." Magellan touched his hand to his forehead and bowed low.

"We're here to sign up for the dance contest," Drew said.

"Of course, I knew that." He slid an entry form to

them. He watched while Sara filled in her information, then passed it on to Drew. "Interesting choice," he murmured.

Sara glanced at him. "You mean the dance contest?"

His smile was inscrutable. "That and other things. Life lends us all interesting choices. We must choose wisely."

Drew slid the form back across the table and took her arm. "Let's go," he said.

She followed him to a place on the edge of the area that had been cleared off for dancing, as far from Magellan as they could get. "That guy gives me the creeps," Drew said.

She laughed. "It's all an act. The mysterious swami."

"He came into the store this morning. Started asking all these personal questions. As if my life is any of his business."

Drew's discomfort amused her. She tried to remember what Magellan had said about him when they played Truth or Bare—but she'd been so preoccupied with the thought of possibly having to take off her clothes in public that she hadn't paid close attention. Whatever it was, the man had evidently touched a nerve. "Come on," she said. "Let's dance. We can warm up for the contest."

She pulled him toward the middle of the floor, where they joined two dozen other couples in shimmying to the latest hip-hop hit. Then, in midsong the tempo switched and a man's bass voice boomed over the speakers. "Are you dancers ready to get your freak on?"

A cheer sounded from the crowd and the music pulsed even louder. "There here we go, for the *Sin on the Beach* Freak Dance Fantasia!"

Drew gaped at Sara. "Freak dancing? This is a freak-dancing contest?"

She laughed. "I guess so."

She looked around at the other couples, who were already getting down, rubbing against one another in a frankly sexual manner.

"Do you know how to do this?" Drew asked.

She shook her head. "But I figure it's a matter of doing what comes naturally." She grinned at him.

He stared at the couple next to them. The woman was grinding her bottom against the man's crotch, while he ran his hands over her breasts. "It's like having sex in public," he said.

"Except with our clothes on." Heat filled her at the idea. In a few days she'd have to return to her ordinary, staid life. Right now she wanted to give free rein to her wild child. She wanted to be daring and outrageous and uninhibited. She put her hands on his shoulders and looked him in the eye, then shimmied the length of his body, rubbing her breasts against his chest, telling him with her eyes exactly what she wanted to do with him.

Heat flared in his eyes and he positioned his thigh between her legs, coming up hard against her sex. The beaded dress slid up her thighs, revealing a swath of naked skin. Drew reached around and grabbed her butt and squeezed, sending a rush of desire straight to her sex.

Ordinary Sara Montgomery didn't behave this way. But the wild Sara she *might* have turned out to be had her life been different intended to seize the moment and enjoy herself. She shimmied up and down his leg, moving in time with the music, refusing to look at anyone but him. The fact that they were not alone here on the floor, that they could ultimately only go so far with this, somehow added to the excitement of the moment.

The music shifted tempo and Drew spun her around, so that her back was to him. She could feel his erection pressed against her, the hard heat of him penetrating the thin fabric of the dress. She bent forward and swayed her butt in time to the hypnotic beat of the music, remembering this afternoon, when they had made love in the locked ladies' room.

He must have been remembering it too. He thrust against her, hands gripping her waist, the frustrating friction of fabric against fabric only making her hotter.

She covered her breasts with her hands and squeezed, trying to ease the ache there. Then she saw a man on the sidelines watching her. He smiled and nodded, then wrote something on the clipboard in his hand. She supposed he was a judge. Did he like that move?

Drew's hands covered hers. "Allow me," he said, bending to whisper in her ear. His palms brushed across her breasts, rubbing the fabric across her sensitive, erect nipples. She swallowed hard, struggling to keep a serene expression on her face. This was insane, carrying on like this in public.

And yet it was exhilarating, too. Erotic and unconventional. All the things she wanted to be.

Drew took her by the arms and turned her to face him once more. "We keep this up, I'm going to come in my pants," he growled, his breath hot in her ear, his voice rough with need.

The idea of him so aroused and ready made her ache to have him inside her. He pulled her close and looked into her eyes. "The minute we get alone, I'm going to hike up that sexy little dress and sink right into you," he whispered.

"Yes." It was more moan than word, and she had to hold on to him to keep from slithering to the ground in a warm, wet puddle. They'd all but stopped dancing now, their bodies pressed together as close as possible, every nerve alert to the next movement, the next brush of a hand or caress of clothing that would wind the tension within that much tighter.

She was so into the moment, so focused on him, that she let out a small scream when someone tapped her on the shoulder. The man with the clipboard stood beside her. "You can go now," he said. "We've chosen our finalists."

"You mean we didn't even get to the finals?" she asked. Obviously, true passion was no judging criteria. She and Drew had generated enough electricity between them to light up half of L.A.

"Sorry, no." The man looked at his clipboard. "Thanks for playing."

She started to argue, but Drew took her arm and dragged her away. "How could we not even be finalists?" she asked. "I thought we were doing pretty good."

"I think we were too into it," he said. "We were making love. The ones who win these things are just dancing."

"Oh." His observation—and his use of the *L*-word silenced her. She watched a leather-clad couple in the middle of the floor. The man had struck a pose and the woman gyrated around him as if he were a stripper's pole. She bent and swayed and licked her lips and the crowd hooted and hollered. It was clear she was performing, not lost to sensation as Sara had been.

"Let's get out of here," Drew said. He wrapped his arm around her and led her off the dance floor. They passed the Sexual Trivia game and Sara looked for Candy, but didn't see her friend. Had she and Matt already been eliminated, or had they been distracted by other activities?

The section of the beach not devoted to the party was dark and all but deserted. Drew stopped and pulled Sara close, in a long, drugging kiss. He tasted of lime and tequila and a sweetness that was simply him. His tongue plunged and retreated in frank imitation of what they both wanted, and she pressed more tightly against him in a silent plea.

When they finally broke apart, she was breathless and lightheaded. "Come back to my place," he said. "Now."

"Yes."

They practically ran to his car, laughing as they

piled in. Before she could even fasten her seatbelt, he'd started the engine and was backing out of the parking space. On the short drive she stared out the window, letting the humid night air rush over her face, imagining how it would feel on her naked skin. She had never felt so sensual, so *womanly*. Every light seemed brighter, every horn honk louder, amplified by a filter of desire.

At Drew's house, they raced each other to the door and up the stairs. She reached his bedroom first and he followed on her heels, shutting the door behind her. Then he grabbed her and pressed her back against the wall, his lips to hers, hungry and demanding.

She responded with the same hunger, arching against him, sliding her hands up under his shirt and raking her nails across his back. She was a wild woman, insatiable, and he responded with a wildness of his own.

She wore a thong under her dress and with one sharp tug he tore it from her and flung it across the room, and shoved her dress up over her hips. The sudden sensation of being naked, exposed, sent a shiver through her. He unzipped his pants and pushed them down with one hand, and she boldly wrapped her hand around his penis, a fresh wave of wet heat concentrating between her legs at the sensation of his iron-hard shaft.

He pulled her to him once more and traced her ear with his tongue. "I want inside you now," he said.

"Yes." She slid her hands up to his shoulders, then

wrapped one leg around his hip. Understanding what she wanted, he cupped her buttocks in his hands and boosted her so she could wrap her other leg around him as well. They stood this way, his cock pressed against her aching sex, looking into each other's eyes. She became aware of the rhythm of his heart in each pulse of his arousal, of the measured pace of his breathing and the strength of his arms holding her. In his gaze she saw the depth of all she felt and hoped and needed.

She smiled, and he smiled in return, and walked slowly to the bed, where he laid her down, then sheathed himself in a condom and slid into her.

She was hot and slick and oh-so-ready for him. She sighed at the pleasure of him filling her completely. "Look at me," he said.

She looked up into his eyes, moved by the frank need she saw in his gaze. "I want to see all of you when you come," he said. "And I want you to see me."

She nodded, and slid her hands up his body, feeling the hard ridge of his torso and the soft hair of his chest against her palms. She brushed against the hard brown nubs of his nipples and heard the sharp intake of his breath. He thrust harder, driving her back on the bed, and she quivered deep in her womb.

"You are so incredibly sexy," he said, caressing her thighs. Then he moved his hand around between them and began to fondle her, very softly at first, then with more pressure as she arched toward him.

He slid almost all the way out of her with agonizing slowness that had her reaching for him, then plunged back into her. Each movement was a little faster than the last, a little stronger, and the tempo of his thumb across her clit mimicked his strokes. The combination stole all speech and coherent thought. She was helpless with need, breathless with wanting, thrilled at the prospect of the pleasure which lay before her.

She kept her eyes open, watching him, seeing him marshal his own desire in favor of her need. The tenderness of this gesture was the push that took her over the edge, into a surging, spiraling climax that sent tears of joy trickling down her face.

"I know," he murmured, wiping the tears, then bringing his thumb to his mouth, tasting them. "I know." Then he followed her to his own release, his face contorted into a picture of strength and vulnerability.

As one, they rolled to their sides and she kept him inside her, maintaining that connection, cradling her head on his shoulder, his arms around her. When he finally did roll over and dispose of the condom, she caressed his back, tracing the bump of each vertebrae. She had never felt as close to anyone as she had with him. She loved how he accepted her in all her moods, whether she was fretting over some business detail with Uncle Spence or falling off a surfboard or playing the wild woman on the dance floor. She could be herself with him, completely, an idea that was as exhilarating as making love with him had been.

He rolled over and held her once more. "You don't mind that we missed most of the party?" he asked.

"I'd rather be with you than at any party."

"I wish we could have spent more time together while you've been here."

"We've done all we could, considering we both have businesses to run." She smoothed her hand down his chest. "Besides, if we spent any more time together, I might not be able to walk."

He laughed. "You have a point." He pulled her closer. "You've been a good influence on me," he said.

"I have?"

"I've been thinking—maybe I will hire someone to help with the book work and stuff at the Surf Shack."

The shift from the discussion of their relationship to talk of hiring a new employee startled her, but she had never claimed to be an expert on how men's minds worked. "That would be good," she said. "It would give you more time for surfing."

"And other things." He smoothed his hand down her arm. "That morning we met, I felt as if I was stuck in my life. Time was passing by, but I wasn't going anywhere."

Magellan's words came back to her now. "You had a hole in your life you were trying to fill."

He nodded. "I know now what I was looking for, and I think I found it in you."

Her throat tightened so she couldn't speak. Instead, she stretched up to kiss him. When their lips parted at last, he brushed back her hair. "Stay with me again tonight," he said.

"Yes." No telling what Candy and Ellie thought of her not coming back to the beach house three nights in a row. She hoped they were cheering for her. Or maybe they were both spending the night with the men in their lives as well. This had been a truly magical trip, with all three of them finding great men. She still remembered the dazed look on Candy's face this afternoon when she'd announced she was in love. How cool would it be if Ellie ended up in love with Bill as well?

As for her and Drew—yes, she was in love with him. The idea both frightened and thrilled her. It was still too soon to make a declaration, but she was sure he felt the same way. He showed her with his every action, even if he had not said the words yet.

She drifted to sleep on this happy thought, and woke hours later to the loud notes of "Bolero." "Is that your phone?" Drew grumbled from beneath the covers on his side of the bed.

"Yes." She sat up and tried to untangle herself from the blankets.

Drew put his arm around her and pulled her back down. "Don't answer it," he said, nuzzling her neck.

She stared toward the table by the door where she'd abandoned her purse last night. She could practically see the purse vibrating with each insistent ring. "I have to," she said. "It's so early. Something might be wrong."

He let her go then. She threw aside the blankets and raced to retrieve the phone from her purse. Heart pounding wildly, she flipped it open. "Hello?"

"Sara! I just had a phone call from Diego Martin. He wants to know why he has to wait until the end of the month to close on the Cummings property."

"What?" She blinked and ran her hand through her hair, and tried to focus her mind on Diego Martin and the Cummings property—not an easy task considering it was six-thirty in the morning and she was sitting on the floor naked while Drew watched from the bed.

"The Cummings property. He wants to close next week instead of the end of the month. Something about a trip he has planned or something."

She rubbed her eyes and stifled a yawn. "He called you at this hour to talk about that?"

"He has business on the east coast, so he was up early to talk to them. Can you move the closing?"

"Tell him the closing is scheduled for the end of the month and it can't be done sooner."

"But surely we could move it up. If you came home and worked on it—"

"Uncle Spence, I'm on vacation." She glanced at Drew. He frowned and sat up on the edge of the bed, the blankets pulled across his lap.

"This is more important than any vacation." Uncle Spence's voice was stern. "Mr. Martin's account is a significant portion of our business. It's not like you to slack off on something like this."

"I'm not slacking," she said, wounded by his words.

She glanced at Drew and he shook his head and mimed hanging up the phone.

She shook her head and tried to focus on what

Uncle Spence was saying. "I'll call Mr. Martin as soon as I get off the phone with you," she said. "I'll see what we can work out. If nothing else, we can put off the closing until he returns from his trip."

"I suggested that, but he says the interest rate he's locked in will expire."

"I'll take care of this, Uncle Spence. I promise. Don't worry." She hung up before he could protest further, and stood. "I have to go now," she said, searching for her clothes. "I'm sorry."

"If you keep running every time he calls, you're never going to have any peace," he said.

"It's my job to take care of these things." She located the ripped thong and stared at it, then tossed it aside and slipped the dress over her head.

"You're on vacation. Can't he handle this for once?"

"He expects me to handle it," she said, her voice muffled by the dress. One last tug got it over her shoulders and she shrugged it in place over her hips and stared at Drew. "You wouldn't turn your back on Gus, would you?"

"Gus would never be so unreasonable," he said. "At least he lets me have a life."

"I have a life," she said. "A good one." But even as she said the words, she realized how much they contradicted the thoughts that had been running through her head off and on all week. She had a busy life. A productive life. A life of responsibility and obligation and always doing the right thing.

But was it a *good* life? Where was the room for dreams and relaxation—and love?

"You could have a better one if you'd stand up to him for a change and stop catering to him," Drew said.

Is that what he'd thought of her all this time—that she was a pushover who let her uncle run her life? "I told you how much I owe Spence. I thought you understood."

"You don't owe him anything anymore."

Pain twisted her stomach as she looked at him. Was this really the tender, caring man who had made love to her last night? "What is wrong with you?" she asked. "I thought you, of all people, understood what it was like to have responsibilities—family obligations."

"But I'm willing to change that, to slow down in order to spend more time with you." He pulled the blankets more tightly around his hips. "I told you I'm thinking of hiring someone to do the book work— so we could have more time together."

"I never asked you to change for me," she said.

"Then change for yourself."

"I thought you understood that you and Spence are *both* important to me." She dug through her purse, searching for a comb, avoiding his gaze. She couldn't believe this was happening. Not now, when everything had been so perfect. "I'm proud of my job. I *like* my work. It's not fair of you to ask me to give it up."

"Don't put words in my mouth." He stood, and had to make a fast grab to keep the blankets from sliding to the floor. "I'm not asking you to give up your job. I'm just asking you to find some balance."

"I'm trying to find balance." Now he wanted her to tilt her life a whole other way—his way. How could she have been so wrong about him?

"You're wrong. You're all out of balance." He took a step toward her, then stopped, as if unwilling to close the gap between them. "I need to know you'll be there for me and you've made it plain you can't be."

How did they get from her rushing to help Spence to her not being there for him? This was spiraling out of control. "I can't talk about this now," she said. She shoved the comb back into her purse and turned away. "I have to go."

"Go then. Go all the way back to L.A. for all I care."

Back to L.A. She stared at him, open-mouthed. Was that it, then? Were all the emotions between them meaningless if Drew couldn't get his way? She closed her mouth then turned and ran down the stairs.

She paused at the door, waiting for him to do or say something—to come to her or to call her back. But silence was like a wall of ice between them. Head down to hide her tears, she left. It was a long walk to the beach house, but maybe that's what she needed—to put some time and distance between herself and the man who had ruined her life...and stolen her heart.

11

"SO SHE LEFT, did she?"

Drew was sitting at the kitchen table, head in his hands, trying to find the energy to get up and pour another cup of coffee, when Gus entered the kitchen. Drew raised his head and looked at his grandfather. The old man was entirely too chipper for someone his age who had been out late last night.

"What are you talking about?" he asked. As if he didn't know.

"You think I didn't hear your big blow-up?" Gus helped himself to coffee and sat across from Drew. "I thought you were crazy about that girl. Why did you let her leave?"

"I didn't *let* her leave. She chose to leave." The knowledge still stung. Sara would rather run off to help her uncle—whom Drew doubted really needed her help—than stay with him.

"You're a fool either way."

Drew glared at his grandfather. "Takes one to know one."

Gus half smiled and nodded. "Want to talk about it?"

"No." Then Drew added, "She was leaving to go

back to work. Some crisis with her uncle." She hadn't said she was going back to L.A., but she hadn't refuted the idea when he'd thrown it out to her.

He'd been stupid, really, blowing up that way over one phone call. But it wasn't simply one phone call. It was Sara always putting her uncle first. Ahead of Drew.

"The man owns the company but he can't do anything without Sara there to hold his hand," he continued, as if he could find some rationalization for his own stupidity. "She's letting him ruin her life, but she can't see that."

"And you can't make her see it." Gus shook his head. "People have to live their own lives, Drew. Make their own mistakes. You can't be responsible for them all the time."

"I can't help it. I'm the responsible type."

"Maybe Sara is, too."

Drew winced. It didn't take a genius to see he and Sara weren't that different. Maybe she had to help her Uncle Spence, the way he had to worry about Gus. Neither one of them made a lot of sense from an outsider's perspective. He could admit he admired her loyalty to Spence, but it didn't take a genius to see how it would always be—Uncle Spence forever interrupting them, Sara always rushing away to do his bidding. Drew got a sick feeling in his stomach whenever he thought of it. Just as well to let her go now and save himself heartache later.

Small comfort, considering how much he hurt now.

"If she's going back to work, I guess she won't be at the surfing competition tomorrow," Gus said.

He'd forgotten about the competition. "I guess she won't be." He frowned at his grandfather. "Are you still planning on giving an exhibition beforehand?"

"You bet." Gus shoved back his chair and stood. "People want to see the three-time world champion show his stuff."

"I wish you wouldn't do it, Grandpa. It's too risky."

"Life is risky, son." Gus leaned toward him, hands on the table. "I know you don't want to hear this, but I'd rather die on a surfboard, doing what I love, than sitting in a chair watching everyone else have fun."

Part of Drew could understand Gus's thinking— but the rest of him couldn't accept his grandfather's decision to take that chance. If someone Drew loved were about to make a big mistake, the least he could do was to try to stop them.

So far, with both Sara and Gus, he was batting zero. Did that mean he should give up?

He stared into his empty coffee cup, as if he might find answers to his questions there. But all he found was an empty cup. As empty as he felt right now.

He closed his eyes and the memory of holding Sara came back to him. He could still feel her on his skin, still smell the scent of her in the air. She was the best thing that had ever happened to him and now she was gone.

Gus might think he was a fool for letting her go, but he didn't see how he could hold someone who didn't want to stay.

BY THE TIME Sara arrived at the beach house, her hair was windblown, her shoes were full of sand and she had a headache from squinting into the sun. Of course Spence called her as she was climbing the steps, to find out why she hadn't called Mr. Martin yet. "I'm sorry, Uncle Spence," she said, trying to be quiet to avoid waking Candy and Ellie. "I promise I'll call. I have to go now." She hung up. Spence understood hang-ups. He'd wait another half hour at least before he tried again. That would give her time to get her head together a little.

She hoped.

She was surprised to find Candy, looking worse for wear, in her sofa bed with a man buried under the covers next to her. At least, that was definitely a male foot resting on the pillow.

"Matt?" Sara whispered.

Candy put a finger to her mouth, gave the man beside her a wary look, then shook her head. She scrambled out and motioned for Sara to join her in the kitchen. Once there she confessed that she and Matt had broken up, then she briefly recounted the rest of her evening. "Listen, can I borrow your laptop?"

Candy had spent the night—in bed—with a guy who wasn't Matt and all she wanted was to borrow a laptop? The poor girl really had lost it if she was worried about work at a time like this. "I guess so," Sara said. She didn't really like to lend her computer, but Candy sounded desperate. Besides, now that things had fallen apart with Drew, Sara might as well go back to L.A. where she had access to computers at the office. "Sure. I'll leave it here." Suddenly she felt overwhelmed. "Look, I've gotta go…."

"Wait. What's wrong?"

She shook her head, but before she could give an excuse for why she didn't want to talk, Ellie—her hair dyed black once more—walked in.

"Hey, girl! What happened to you two?"

Candy went through the shushing routine again, then had to explain to Ellie what had happened and reassure her that she'd done nothing to precipitate the break-up. In a clear attempt to bolster the flagging team morale, Candy volunteered to work on the contest essay. She promised to deliver one guaranteed to clench the grand prize for them.

While Sara wanted her friends to win, she knew she would never make use of the time-share beach house. To do so she would risk running into Drew and she didn't have the heart for that.

Candy started concocting a hangover cure and Sara went into her bedroom to pack. Now that she'd made up her mind, she was anxious to leave as quickly as possible. Maybe she thought if she moved fast enough, she could outrun the hurt that dragged at her. Or maybe it was only that every minute she was here on the beach was another minute of re-membering all the good times she'd shared with Drew, and the horrible way they'd parted.

She opened her suitcase on the bed and dumped in the contents of the dresser drawers, then began gathering items from the bathroom. She tossed items in haphazardly. If she forgot anything, Ellie and Candy would bring it home for her.

When she emerged from the bedroom a few minutes later, suitcase in hand, Ellie nodded to Sara's suitcase. "Where are you going?"

"Are you moving to Drew's place?" Candy asked. She looked a little perkier now, though she still wore last night's dress and her hair was a mess, much as Sara's was.

Sara shook her head. "I'm going home," she said.

"Home?" Ellie looked alarmed. "Why? Is something wrong?"

"An emergency at work I need to take care of."

"Uncle Spence finally wore you down," Candy said knowingly.

"He sounded on the verge of a nervous breakdown when he called," Sara said. "According to him, without me there the company is on the brink of collapse."

"I think he might be exaggerating a little, don't you?" Candy said.

"I wonder if he's feeling bad because he's not getting his coffee the way he likes it," Ellie said.

"It doesn't matter why he's feeling this way, I have to go." Sara started to move past them, but Ellie stopped her.

"Hon, this is your vacation," she said. "You can't leave early. What about Drew?"

"We already said goodbye," she said.

Candy and Ellie exchanged looks. Sara had hoped they'd be satisfied with this simple explanation, but of course they weren't. "What happened?" Candy said. "I thought you two were getting along."

"We were." Sara stared at the floor, trying to find words to describe something that still made no sense. "Everything was going great, and then this morning, when Uncle Spence called—" She gripped the handle of the suitcase harder. "I don't know what happened. Drew just…I told him I had to leave to help Uncle Spence and he took it that I was leaving *him,* and one thing led to another—I thought he'd understand. After all, he looks after his grandfather and his grandfather's business. But it was almost as if he was *jealous* of Uncle Spence."

"Aww, hon." Ellie moved closer and rubbed Sara's shoulder. "Maybe he *was* jealous. Maybe he thought you were choosing Spence over him."

"But that's ridiculous," she said. "I love Spence, but in a different way than I love Drew."

"So you really love him." Candy let out a heavy sigh. "Join the club."

Sara nodded. She had heard the cliché about love hurting but she'd never expected pain like this. "It was awful," she said. "He said I'd proved I couldn't be there for him." She bit her lip, fighting tears. All this time she'd managed to avoid crying, but Candy and Ellie's sympathy was too much. She wanted to curl up in a corner and bawl.

She straightened her shoulders. "I guess I'd better go. Uncle Spence is expecting me."

"Don't go," Ellie said. "I know you want to help. The thing I'm starting to figure out is that sometimes the best way to help someone is not to rush in to look after everything for them, but to let them help themselves."

It was Sara and Candy's turn to stare at Ellie. She looked sheepish. "I know. I'm always looking after people. But now it's time to look after myself. Maybe it's time for you to do that, too, Sara."

"You needed this vacation more than any of us," Candy said. "If you leave now, you'll be missing out on so much. Not just Drew."

"And what about the surfing competition?" Ellie asked. "Isn't that tomorrow?"

Sara nodded. "I know you were counting on me to earn more points for our competition, but I don't know if I can do it without Drew there to help me."

"You can do it," Candy said. "You can get out there and show him how good you are. Remind him you're a strong woman who can make her own choices."

"And we really do need the points," Ellie said.

Sara looked down at her suitcase. If she went home now, Uncle Spence would be grateful, and she'd avoid the guilt she was sure to feel if she left him on his own—even if he did manage to muddle through this crisis by himself. On the other hand, she'd have to deal with wondering what would have happened had she stayed here. Could she have won the surfing competition? Had she let her friends down?

She looked up at Candy and Ellie, who watched her with hope in their eyes. "All right," she said. "I'll stay. At least until after the surfing competition. I don't want to let you down."

"You're not letting us down, either way," Ellie said, hugging her close. "And a certain hunky surfer might be at the competition."

"I don't know if I want to see him again," she said. Even as she said the words, a voice inside her head whispered *Liar!* More than anything, she wished this morning had never happened, and that she and Drew were still happy together. But she of all people knew wishing alone didn't change anything. She needed both Drew and Uncle Spence in her life, but Drew couldn't accept that.

"Maybe it's just as well I've never had a serious relationship with a man," she said. "It complicates things too much. Honestly, who has time these days for work and family *and* a man? I should have stuck with my original plan and only had a vacation fling."

"Don't be so hard on yourself," Candy said. "Sometimes these things happen. Look at me and Matt. I certainly never intended to fall in love with the man. He's my boss—what could be more inconvenient?"

Inconvenient. Yeah. To most people, Uncle Spence needing her to handle a crisis at work would be inconvenient. To Drew it was impossible. "I guess whatever feelings we had between us couldn't stand up to the real world," she said.

Ellie hugged her. "Love is a bitch sometimes. I know you're hurt, but I'm glad you're staying. Later, we'll drown your sorrows properly. Right now, I have to get to the set."

"Say hello to Bill for us," Candy said. She turned back to Sara. "You okay?"

Sara nodded. "I'll live."

"Then I'm going to take a quick shower and get to work."

"I think I'll take a surfboard out and get some practice," Sara said. "If I'm going to compete in the contest tomorrow, I still need to work." She needed to get out of the house, away from the phone and Uncle Spence's pleading. She also needed to be busy doing something besides replaying the last half hour with Drew over and over and over. What could she have done differently? What could she have said differently?

Such questions were useless. Real life had come up against real love and love had taken a beating. Or maybe it was only that beach romances were never meant to thrive away from the sand and surf.

Sara returned her suitcase to the bedroom and changed into a bikini. She chose the blue one, avoiding the orange one she'd worn the first day—the day she and Drew met.

No, she wasn't going to think about him right now. There was another surf shop down the beach. She'd rent a board from them and practice the moves Drew had shown her, doing her best not to remember the happy hours they'd spent in and out of the water.

Her phone rang. She checked her watch and saw it was almost exactly thirty minutes since she'd last spoken to Uncle Spence. The man was nothing if not predictable. She flipped open the phone. "Hello, Uncle Spence."

"Sara, did you call Martin yet?"

She took a deep breath, remembering everything she'd said to Candy and Ellie. "No, I haven't. I need you to call him. If he objects, tell him I'm on vacation. Everyone's entitled to a vacation."

Silence. She'd so seldom spoken to him this way, she could tell he was stunned. "Sara," he said finally. "Responsibilities come before personal pleasure."

She cut off a sigh. "Uncle Spence, I know you taught me to be responsible. I promised my room-mates here that I'd help them with a big project and I can't let them down."

"And what about Martin?"

"Tell him to call his bank to ask for an extension on his interest rate, then tell him to have a nice trip and we'll do the closing when he returns."

She thought she heard a chuckle. "You're a very smart young woman."

Her shoulders sagged with relief. She'd been deter-mined to hold her ground, no matter what, but she was relieved he wasn't angry. "I learned from the best."

He hesitated, then added, "And you do deserve this vacation. I know you work hard. Maybe too hard. You've made it so easy for me to depend on you and I guess I take advantage of that sometimes."

She smiled. If she'd been with him, she'd have given him a big hug and a kiss. Instead, she settled for this parting reassurance. "I'll call later to find out how everything went."

"I could call you—"

"I'm going to be busy and I'll have my phone off."
She needed a break. "I promise I'll check in with you."

"All right, dear. I'll let you go now. Enjoy the rest
of your vacation."

She hung up the phone, feeling weepy all over
again. Uncle Spence was such a dear, sweet soul.
He'd helped her regain confidence in herself at a
time in her life when she'd felt lost.

As for enjoying the rest of her vacation, that didn't
seem possible without Drew. But she still had Candy
and Ellie to cheer her on. And she had the knowledge
that she'd been in tough spots before and had come
out okay. When she was a teenager, Uncle Spence
had helped her, but surely she was old enough now
to help herself.

She'd show up for the surfing competition
tomorrow and do her best. She'd prove Drew a good
teacher, whether he was there to see her or not.

DREW FORCED HIMSELF to go into work, telling
himself keeping busy was the best way to get through
the pain of losing Sara. But even at the Surf Shack,
he was tortured by his emotions. The weathered
building filled with surfing gear wasn't just a place
of business to him—it was part of his family history.
He'd all but grown up behind the counter and in the
back room. As a baby, he'd stacked cans of surf wax
instead of wooden blocks, and he'd learned to count
by operating the cash register.

Everything in his family, from when they ate

dinner to how they celebrated holidays, revolved around the Surf Shack. There were times when Drew had felt like the luckiest kid in the world growing up here, and times when he'd absolutely hated it.

He studied the pictures on the wall beside the door and zeroed in on an old Christmas card that pictured him, his mom and dad and Gus, each wearing a Santa hat and posing with a surfboard. Merry Christmas from the Surf Shack read the caption. Not from the Jamisons or even Dot, Jeff, Gus and Drew. But from the Surf Shack.

He hadn't been completely honest with Sara when he'd told her he'd become an insurance adjuster as a way of rebelling. He'd done it to try to escape the thing he'd seen as his rival for his parents' and grandfather's affections. The Surf Shack was their pride and joy, their focus in life. Drew had reasoned that moving into another way of life altogether would force his family to see him as an individual.

To acknowledge that he was more important to them than a business.

And then Gus had had his heart attack and Drew had realized that while his family loved the Surf Shack, they loved each other more. Their business had allowed them to work together, doing what they loved, but they had been willing to give it up if it would keep Gus around a little longer.

He turned away from the photographs, and walked to the picture window that overlooked the pier and the ocean beyond. When Sara had said she was rushing off to help her Uncle Spence, it had been as if Drew were ten years old again, denied a trip to Disney World because summer was the busiest time at the store.

He'd behaved with all the maturity of a ten-year-old, too, he thought ruefully. Or a two-year-old. He'd all but lain on the floor and kicked his heels, demanding Sara drop everything to cater to him.

Why did such insights always come too late?

And now she'd gone back to L.A. Chased there by him. He'd blown it. He considered asking Gus what to do, but feared another philosophical lecture on life as related to surfing or the ocean or grains of sand or some such. Too many minutes into such speeches and Drew's head began to hurt. The old man meant well, but what Drew needed right now was clear directions.

What he needed was Sara. It took her leaving for him to realize how much.

SARA WAS SURPRISED by how much better she felt once she was in the water. Not that being there didn't make her remember every moment she'd spent with Drew, but the rhythm of the waves and the physical exertion of remembering everything she was supposed to do to surf them had a calming effect.

She'd just completed her second successful attempt at riding a wave when a beefy guy with a dark tan, long blond hair and a sunburst tattoo on the right side of his chest paddled near and hailed her. "You looked good out there," he said.

"Thanks." She flung herself back onto her board,

a move she was convinced no amount of experience would make graceful. "I'm learning."

"I could give you a few pointers, if you like." His teeth were blindingly white against his tan. And she couldn't help noticing his gaze was focused somewhere in the vicinity of her chest.

"Thanks, but I don't want to keep you," she said, trying for a brush-off that wouldn't be too rude—something else she doubted could be accomplished gracefully.

"It's no trouble." He paddled closer. "What you want to do is get your right foot a little farther forward. That'll help with your balance."

Okay, so maybe he did know something about surfing. His advice made sense. It sounded like something Drew might have told her.

"Thanks," she said. "I'll give it a try."

"And don't be afraid to be aggressive. You want to resist the water, not just let the wave toss you around."

She nodded. "Okay."

"I'm Garth," he said, flashing another blinding grin.

"Sara."

"You live around here?"

She shook her head. "Do you?"

"Nah, I'm just up for the weekend, visiting some friends. I'm from Santa Monica."

"I'm from L.A."

"Then we're practically neighbors."

Not the most brilliant pickup line she'd ever heard, but not totally lame, either. The truth was, he seemed like a nice guy. Good-looking, probably fun to be with.

The kind of guy she *should* have hooked up with for a vacation fling instead of someone like Drew, who'd set her heart to racing the moment she laid eyes on him.

Unfortunately, she was in no mood now to flirt it up with anyone. "It was nice meeting you," she said. "And thanks for the tip. But I'd better get back to practicing. I'm entered in a competition tomorrow and I have a lot of work to do to get ready."

"The *Sin on the Beach* festival?" He grinned. "Me too. Some friends of mine are trying to collect points to win a stay in a beach house or something and they talked me into helping them out."

Had he said he was from Santa Monica? "So you're just here for the surfing competition?" she asked.

"That's right. They figured if they were going to win, they'd better bring in someone who knew what he was doing."

"Right." She paddled farther away from him. "Guess I'd better go. See ya."

"Yeah. See you around."

She ducked under an approaching wave and paddled toward the next swell. Santa Monica. She'd bet money Garth was there as a ringer for the team that had been beating her and Ellie and Candy all week.

Of course, nothing in the rules said a team couldn't add members at the last minute. But it felt like cheating to her. All week the Santa Monica bunch had proved they'd do anything to win.

She timed the approaching swell, then turned her

board to angle on it. Focusing everything she had on the moment, she heaved herself to her feet, stepping farther forward this time, as Garth had suggested. She could feel the wave thrusting against the board, lifting her, and she extended her arms to balance and thought about the idea of resisting the push of the water. With the slightest shift of her body, she was able to angle the board along the wave, the roar of the surf in her ears, the wind blowing her hair back. She felt lighter than air, incredibly free and powerful. She wanted to shout for joy, so she did, confident no one would hear her over the surf.

Why couldn't she be that free in her everyday life? She rode the wave out, then sank into the water and floated for a long while, using her board as a raft. She squinted at the sky overhead and thought of Uncle Spence. She'd spent so many years bending over backward to prove she was worthy of the chance he'd taken on her. And in the end neither she nor Spence was very happy with the results. She felt overworked and stretched thin by his demands, and Spence seemed as stressed as ever.

And she'd had the nerve to worry about the Santa Monica team cheating. All these years, she'd been cheating herself and Uncle Spence. She'd cheated herself out of the full life she should have been living.

She was still upset with Drew for getting angry when she'd chosen to help Uncle Spence rather than stay with him, but she could admit now he'd been right when he'd argued she was spending too much of her time trying to smooth the way for Uncle Spence. Her life *was* out of balance. For that matter, so was Spence's.

So what was she going to do about it? So far she'd been drifting along, letting life happen to her, instead of making things happen for herself.

A flutter of excitement worked its way through her as she began paddling toward the beach. She'd tried a lot of new things this week: surfing, freak-dancing, body-painting. Time to take that spirit of adventure away from the beach into real life. Time to stop going with the flow and get a little aggressive.

12

DREW DEBATED staying away from the beach
Saturday morning. He could use the excuse he
needed to look after the Surf Shack, but the truth
was he didn't think his nerves could stand
watching his grandfather for signs of ill health and
constantly checking the crowd for Sara. Yes, she
had said she was leaving, but he couldn't shake the
hope that she would be there. She'd seemed
serious about wanting to win points for her team,
and she'd worked hard to improve her technique.
Would she really throw all that away to handle
some business deal?

In the end, he couldn't stay away. He left Cooter
behind the counter and joined the crowd around the
bleachers that had been set up on the sand. Giant
speakers blared the Beach Boys and various surfing
tunes and colorful streamers popped in the stiff
breeze. The air smelled of suntan lotion and roasting
hot dogs from the refreshment wagon.

He made his way through the shoulder-to-
shoulder mob to the area set aside for competition
officials. When a burly guy with a crewcut tried to

stop him, Drew did a double take. "Moose, it's me, Drew. Has Gus done his thing yet?"

Morris "Moose" Gibson, a regular on the local surfing scene, shook his head. "Not yet. But he's already in the water, so I guess that means he's up soon."

Drew shaded his eyes with his hand and scanned the waves. The wind had picked up and the water was a little rough. Several surfers with boards floated in the chop, but from this distance, he couldn't tell which one was his grandfather.

"Dudes and dudettes, we've got a special treat for you this morning before our *Sin on the Beach* surf competition takes place." An announcer interrupted the music and temporarily silenced the crowd. "Gus Jamison, three-time World Champion Surfer has agreed to come out of retirement to show us some of his winning moves. So give it up for Grandpa Gus!"

The crowd cheered and whooped as the opening riff of "Wipe Out" filled the air. Drew's stomach clenched as he zeroed in on a solitary surfer paddling out toward the waves. Gus wore bright-orange trunks and a yellow rash guard, and was using his favorite blue-and-white Whiplash board.

"He looks good out there," Moose said. "Strong paddler for seventy."

Drew nodded and tried to relax, but he felt cold in spite of the sweat trickling down his back.

Gus waited through one set of waves and then another. The volume of chatter from the crowd rose as they grew restless. "He's waiting for his best shot," Drew said out loud. "He wants a good wave to show off."

"Here comes one now," Moose said.

Sure enough, a swell larger than the preceding two was shaping up in the distance. Drew's body tensed as he calculated the speed and angle of the wave along with Gus. His grandfather's timing was perfect as he took his position just ahead of the wave and was lifted by it.

Drew's own leg muscles ached as Gus leaped to his feet, knees bent, arms akimbo, braced on the board. He rode across the face of the wave, then back, zigzagging, the board dipping and diving. The crowd cheered, and Drew realized he was shouting along with them. For all his fear for his grandfather, he recognized the joy of the moment, too. Surfing was part of Gus—like his handlebar moustache and sideburns. Maybe nothing—even a longer life out of the water—was worth asking Gus to give up that essential part of himself.

"Go, Gus!" He screamed, clapping his hands. Exhilaration filled him, as if he were there on the board with his grandfather, enjoying that beautiful ride.

Gus rode the wave all the way to the shallows, and dismounted with the flair and style that had helped him win championships all those years ago. As the crowd continued to applaud and the announcer regaled them with a list of Gus's many accomplishments and awards, Drew raced out to meet him.

The two men embraced, standing in thigh-high water, pushed and buffeted by the surf. Gus was breathing hard, but his color was good, and his spirits were sky-high. "Do I still have it, or what?"

"You still have it, Grandpa," Drew said.

"I could give plenty of these younger guys a run for their money," he said, grinning. His moustache dripped with seawater and his belly sagged beneath the rash guard, but his face glowed with the joy Drew could still feel.

"If they're smart, they won't bother to challenge you," Drew said. "You're still the best."

Gus laughed. "Just as well. I think I only have one run like that in me today." He bent to unfasten the leash of his board.

"Let me get that," Drew said. He unclipped the leash and hefted the board up under his arm.

"Gus, can we have a picture?" One of half a dozen reporters called from the edge of the water.

"Sure thing." Gus put his arm around Drew. "Take a picture of me with my grandson. He's a surfer, too."

Cameras whirred and buzzed like a sudden invasion of locusts. Gus and Drew grinned at the photographers, and at each other, then started toward the judge's stand where Gus would view the competition. Someone handed Gus a bottle of water, and someone else draped a towel around his shoulders. "Awesome ride, dude," Moose said.

A girl in a purple string bikini asked for his autograph, while a blonde in an orange maillot posed for a snapshot with him. Gus's grin was wider than ever. Drew couldn't remember when he'd seen his grandfather so happy.

"I'm sorry I tried to stop you from doing this," Drew said when they reached the judge's stand. "I know how much this means to you. It's the same way I feel when I've had a really good day in the water."

Gus patted his shoulder. "I understand why you tried to stop me. And maybe you were even right. But I wouldn't trade the high I get from being on a board in the water for an infinite number of hours left to me sitting in a chair."

Drew nodded.

Gus accepted a clipboard and a pair of binoculars from a woman who wore a *Sin on the Beach* hoodie over her bikini. "You'd better go and let me get to work," he said. He glanced at the clipboard. "The first heat is the newcomers' division." His eyebrows rose. "Says here that Sara's checked in. She's number four on the lineup."

Drew's heart stuttered in its rhythm. "Sara's here?" he repeated dumbly.

Gus nodded and sat back in his chair. "I'm ready when you are," he told the girl in the hoodie. "Drew, you'd better get back down to the beach."

Numb, Drew made his way down the stairs and into the crowd. The announcer was droning on about the rules of the competition and what the crowd should look for, but the words barely registered with Drew. His mind was too full of Sara—the way she'd looked in his arms the night before last, the dimple that formed on the left side of her mouth when she smiled, the long smooth stretch of her neck when she threw back her head and laughed.

The hurt in her eyes when she'd left him yesterday morning.

The memory hit him like a punch in the gut. He'd been wrong about his grandfather—and he'd been wrong about Sara too. Her choosing to put her uncle first yesterday morning wasn't really all that different from his own commitment to Gus. It didn't mean she didn't have room in her life for him, too.

There was still a chance they could work things out—if he hadn't screwed things up so badly she never wanted to see him again.

WHEN SARA checked in at the area set aside for the contestants of the surfing competition, "Wipeout" was blaring from the loud speakers. She was issued a number to pin to her swimsuit, a free *Sin on the Beach* T-shirt and a goodie bag containing sunscreen, surf wax, lip balm, stickers and other swag from competition sponsors. "Your heat is first," the organizer told her. "Stay close and we'll tell you when to go in the water. I'm guessing in about twenty or thirty minutes."

Raucous cheering from the crowd distracted them and the man looked out at the water. "Get a load of this dude," he said. "Can you believe he's seventy?"

Sara realized the man riding the wave was Gus himself. He zigzagged back and forth across the face of a good-size wave, wowing the crowd. She grinned. "Go, Gus!" She joined in the cheers as he rode his board all the way to the shallows. Watching him out there, having such a good time, made her feel better.

She hoped Drew was here, watching his grandfather. She understood his worry over Gus's health, but as a surfer himself, Drew could surely grasp the joy being here today gave Gus. As Gus finished his ride and came into shore, she lost sight of him, the crowd along the beach blocking her view.

She searched next for Drew, but had no luck picking him out of the mass of people who crowded the bleachers and the beach around them. The surfing competition was proving to be one of the biggest draws of the festival.

The idea of so many people watching her surf—possibly watching her fall off her board, or seeing her fail to get up on it at all—made her stomach hurt. She also had to pee. Looking around, she spotted a row of portable toilets near the parking lot. "May I leave my board here a minute?" she asked the guy behind the registration desk.

He shrugged. "I don't care."

She propped the board next to a stack of chairs, then scooted to the facilities. She had to wait for one to empty, by which time she was practically hopping up and down.

A few minutes later, much relieved, she stepped out, and almost collided with a man in orange trunks and a yellow rash guard. "Gus!" she said, steadying herself against him.

"Sara!" He grinned at her. "Are you ready to ride this morning?"

"I hope so." Her stomach fluttered and she quickly changed the subject. "I saw you just now. You were fantastic out there."

"Thank you. Best ride I've had in a long time."
His expression grew serious. "Hey, aren't you
supposed to be with the contestants for the first
heat?"

"I just had to run to the little girls' room." She
put one hand to her stomach, which was still
jumping around as if she'd swallowed a live fish.
"You know, nerves."

He nodded. "You'll do fine. But I'm saying that
as a friend, you understand. Not as a judge. Up
there—" he pointed toward the judging stand "—I
have to be impartial."

"I know."

"It's good to see you," he said. "Drew was under
the impression you were going back to L.A. Something about an emergency with your uncle."

She flushed. So Drew had confided in Gus. That
was only natural, she supposed. She only hoped he
hadn't said anything too awful about her. "Uncle
Spence was upset about some things, but I managed
to calm him down." She tried for a hearty smile. "I
couldn't let all those surfing lessons go to waste."

"I'm glad you stayed." He laced his hands
together over his stomach and regarded her with a
fond look. "You've been really good for my
grandson, you know. He's been much more relaxed
these last few days with you in the picture."

His words puzzled her. Had Drew *not* told Gus
about their fight? "I'm glad you think that," she said.
"But the truth is, Drew and I had a…disagreement
yesterday morning. We—" She looked away. "I

guess we both said some things we shouldn't have."
But once those things had been said, how did you
take them back?

"I'd say Drew's anger was a good sign," Gus said.

She stared at him. "Why would you think that? He
was really upset." She swallowed hard. "He told me
if I left he couldn't trust me to be there for him."

"Drew doesn't bother getting upset about unim-
portant things," Gus said. "For instance, he hardly
ever loses his temper over things like lost orders or
screw-ups at the Surf Shack. But he pitched a fit
over me surfing again."

"Yes, he told me the two of you had argued
about that."

"I knew it was only because he loves me and cares
about what happens to me." His smile was kind.
"Maybe he's angry with you for the same reason."

"Will the contestants for the first heat please
enter the water?" The announcement blared over
the loudspeaker.

"You'd better go," Gus said. "Good luck."

She hurried to retrieve her board and join the four
others in the newcomers' division in the water. But
all the while, Gus's words echoed in her head.

Drew loved her.

Yes, he'd said so, but only in the aftermath of
lovemaking, when passion could carry anyone away.
Hearing this bold statement from Gus in the cold
light of day made her truly believe the words, as if
for the first time.

The coordinator had explained that they were

each to have a chance to ride a wave and show their stuff for the judges and the audience. As rank amateurs, they'd be rated on form and style like the other more experienced competitors, but would not be expected to execute any fancy tricks. This was simply a chance for beginning surfers to get their feet wet, so to speak, in competitive surfing.

The first contestant, a young man, attacked a swell with enthusiasm, paddling furiously toward the wave, but standing too soon and getting flipped off his board before he could find his balance. A loud *"Awww"* broadcast over the loudspeaker, adding to his humiliation. But when he popped his head above the water and waved that he was all right, the crowd cheered.

The next surfer was a stocky blond in red trunks. When he turned to wave to the crowd, Sara stared at the sunburst tattoo on the right side of his chest. Garth was no beginning surfer, but he was pretending to be one today, no doubt for the benefit of his friends' team.

As "Surfin' U.S.A." blared from the speakers, Garth entered the wave smoothly and quickly stood on his board. He even managed to salute to the crowd as he surfed all the way across the wave, riding it out. The crowd greeted him with cheers while Sara fumed. Couldn't the judges see this was no amateur?

The third surfer did well also, though not as well as Garth. By the time it was Sara's turn, she was taking deep breaths, somewhere between hyperventilating and achieving a semblance of calm. As the first woman in the competition so far, she received a rousing cheer from the crowd. Then she shut out the noise, turning her back on the crowd and paddling toward an incoming wave.

Everything Drew had told her about surfing came back to her now. She could almost hear his voice in her head, telling her how to judge the height and speed of the wave, coaching her on when to turn, when to make her move.

She wobbled a little getting up on her board, and had to fight for balance, but in a split-second she righted herself. "Wa-hoo!" Exhilaration bubbled out of her as she rode the wave. She felt on top of the world, young and free and confident.

The ride was over too soon, and she was sinking into the water, kicking off the board and letting it float behind her. She dunked her head under and came up again, slicking her hair back. The water was warm around her, holding her up and caressing her. She wanted to stay out here a little longer, savoring this feeling of being so carefree.

To think when they'd first arrived in Malibu, sitting on the deck with her computer had held a greater attraction than being in the water this way!

These past few days had changed her so much. Not only had she learned to surf and broken her dating drought, but she really had achieved her goal of rediscovering the free spirit inside her that she'd lost as a girl.

She'd focused for so long on the debt she owed Uncle Spence when any reasonable person would have accepted that their accounts were squared. She did so not because she truly owed Spence, but because it was easier—safer—to tell herself she had to cater to his every whim than to chart her own course for her life.

Years ago, when she'd tried to make her own way, she'd gotten into trouble. But she was a different woman now, one with more experience under her belt and the ability—the wisdom even—to make her own choices.

She thought back to the afternoon she'd declined to go parasailing with Drew because she avoided risk. How silly that seemed now. Why hadn't she seen the difference between the foolish risks she'd made as a teen—taking drugs, hanging out with a rough crowd—and the risks that added excitement and fun to life? Risks like parasailing, surfing…and allowing herself to fall in love.

It was time for the next heat to begin and she had to leave the water and join her fellow competitors on the beach. They stood a little apart from one another on the sand, awaiting the verdict of Gus and the other judges.

"You were really good out there," the first surfer in their heat said to Garth. "You sure you haven't surfed before?"

Garth shook his head. "No, dude. Just started this week."

"That's not what you told me yesterday." Sara positioned herself alongside Garth, who had the grace to look sheepish.

"Aww, I was just mouthing off," he said. "Trying to impress a hot chick."

Sara glared at him, refusing to be swayed by his flattery. He turned away, and began talking to the first surfer about the festival.

Finally one of the contest coordinators made his way toward them. Sara was stunned to see Drew walking with the man. "This is Drew Jamison, from the Surf Shack, one of our sponsors," the coordinator introduced him. "He's here to hand out the awards."

Drew avoided Sara's gaze, but she couldn't stop looking at him. He looked so good. It was all she could do not to throw her arms around him. Instead, she held onto her board tightly, trusting it to keep her upright.

First place went to Garth. No surprise there, Sara thought. His friends cheered and swarmed around him, offering their congratulations. They were all members of the Santa Monica team. Sara glared at them and debated voicing her suspicions that Garth was no amateur. But how could she prove it? She hadn't actually seen him surf yesterday. Maybe he had merely been trying to impress her, though she had her doubts.

Second place was awarded to surfer number five. Sara had been so caught up in enjoying the afterglow of her own ride that she hadn't paid any attention to him. But she could own up to a pinch of disappointment that she hadn't been judged worthy of second place.

"Our third place winner of three hundred points is Sara Montgomery," the coordinator read from his clipboard.

Sara let out a squeal of surprise and delight, but

quickly sobered when Drew approached her with the envelope with her winning certificate. "Hello, Drew," she said, surprised at how normal her voice sounded.

"Hello, Sara." He handed her the envelope. "Congratulations. You looked good out there."

"You were watching?" The knowledge made her feel warm clear through.

He nodded. "You looked like you were having a good time."

"I was." She took a deep breath, then added. "I was remembering all the good times we had together, when you were teaching me."

He looked away. "Yeah."

The silence stretched between them. The other surfers and the coordinator had already wandered away.

Sara couldn't stand it any longer. Maybe she and Drew had both said things they couldn't take back, but she owed it to herself to at least *try* to make things right again. "I—"

"Listen, can we—"

They both laughed nervously. "You first," Drew said.

"I was just going to ask if there was somewhere we could go and talk. Alone," she said.

"Yeah," he said. "I'd like that."

13

DREW NODDED down the beach. "Want to go for a walk?"

"What about my surfboard?" Sara asked.

"We can leave it at the judging booth. Gus will keep an eye on it."

Without her asking, he picked up the board and they set out. She was reminded of the day they'd met, when they'd strolled together in a similar fashion. Had it really only been five days ago? Five days in which so much had changed.

"I saw Gus surfing," she said after a moment. "He looked great out there."

"He did." Drew glanced at her. "I was really pissed off at him for agreeing to do it. I thought he was taking a foolish risk."

"And now what do you think?"

"When I saw him out there, everything *I* feel when I'm on a board came back to me. And I thought of what it would be like if someone told me I could never experience that feeling again." He shook his head. "I guess I was pretty arrogant, thinking because Gus is older he wouldn't feel the loss of something he loves. Now I'm glad he didn't have to give it up. At least not yet."

"I'm just a beginner, but I know a little of what you're talking about," she said. "This morning, when I was out in the water, for those few moments I was riding that wave, it was as if I didn't have a problem in the world. I was truly free." She laughed. "I didn't want to come out of the water."

He glanced at her. "When you left yesterday, I thought you were going back to L.A. What happened?"

"I went back to the beach house and packed. Ellie and Candy were there and they gave me a hard time about leaving."

"So they talked you into staying." His voice was tense, and she could almost hear the words he didn't bother to add: *You wouldn't stay behind when I asked.*

"It wasn't just them," she said. "They reminded me of why I'd come to Malibu in the first place."

"Why was that?"

"I hadn't had a real vacation in, well, forever." She laughed. "They convinced me I was on my way to becoming a colorless drone. If I wanted to save myself from a lifetime of blue suits and microwave dinners for one, I had to get away from the computer for a week and rediscover my inner wild child."

"And did you find her?"

"I found something better." She hesitated, then took his arm and leaned close to him. "I found a wild woman who realized my girlhood dream of learning to surf *and* who fell in love with a truly wonderful man."

He stumbled, then stopped altogether and turned to face her. "Yesterday, you sounded like you were willing to turn your back on all that and go back to L.A. as if nothing had changed."

She nodded. "I was. Then I realized if I did that, this whole vacation had been wasted." She took his hand. "I love Uncle Spence. And I will always feel an obligation to him. But after you and I argued yesterday, I finally realized something that maybe you'd been trying to tell me all along."

"What was that?"

"That what I saw as my debt to him was my own fear in disguise. I was afraid of making decisions in life because I'd screwed up so badly before. It was easier to let Uncle Spence call all the shots. I could feel good about helping him, when really I was only avoiding having my own life." She smiled. "Thanks for helping me see that, even if it did take a while for the realization to sink in."

"I was wrong, too," he said. "I rearranged my whole life to look after Grandpa and then I had the nerve to complain about you wanting to help your uncle."

"I know you only did it because you saw what I was throwing away to run to help a man who actually needed me to step back and let him look after himself."

"That's not entirely true," he said.

"What do you mean?"

"I really did resent your devotion to your job, and to a lesser extent, Uncle Spence. It reminded me of when I was growing up. The Surf Shack always came first for my family. When you talked about leaving because you were needed at work, I was suddenly a little kid again, resenting always being in second place."

"Oh, Drew! I didn't mean it like that."

"I know you didn't. And I felt really stupid, once I realized what was going on. Can you forgive me for being an idiot?"

"If you'll forgive me for being a coward."

"There's nothing to forgive." He pulled her close.

"Are we a pair or what?" Sara asked. She looked him in the eye. This time he didn't turn away.

"I'd say we're a perfect pair," he said. Then he kissed her, and she wanted to shout with relief, even as she melted against him. His lips never leaving hers, he lowered the surfboard to the ground, then wrapped his arms around her, as if he was determined, this time, never to let her get away again.

After a long while, they parted again. "I always feel so right when I'm in your arms," she said. "I felt that way from the first."

"Me, too," he said. "I've never been one to believe in fate and all that, but maybe the two of us really were meant to be together."

"You know I have to go back to L.A. next week to work," she said.

He nodded. "I know. We'll work something out. I'll come visit you there. You can come here. We'll play it by ear." He grinned. "I promise, no more temper tantrums. I'm done with that."

"I have some ideas for making things easier on us," she said. She squeezed his hand. "I don't want to jinx it by speaking too soon. But I have some ideas I think might work out."

He nodded. "I can't wait to hear them. In the meantime…" He slid his hands to her bottom and pulled her snug against him. "Want to go back to my place?"

She laughed. "I've always heard make-up sex is pretty fantastic."

"I'm up for finding out if you are."

They left the surfboard at the judging stand, then drove to Drew's house. Coming here now, in the middle of the day, felt so different to Sara. Or maybe it was only that things were different between her and Drew now. They loved each other. They were talking about the future. She couldn't wait to see what that future held for them.

The urgency that had been a hallmark of their lovemaking before was replaced by a luxurious languor, as if their bodies, too, realized they had all the time in the world to enjoy each other.

They undressed slowly, watching the play of light on each other's skin. Drew put on music to drown out the sound of traffic below, and they danced, naked, around the bedroom—not freak-dancing, but slow-dancing in each other's arms, relishing the brush of thigh to thigh, of breast to chest.

"There's a place I know," he said. "A little cove no one ever goes to. I'll take you there some time and we'll go skinny-dipping."

She loved the idea that they had things to look forward to. "We'll go to County Line Beach one day," she said. "We'll take our boards and go surfing, the way I always wanted to do when I was a girl, but never did." But this would be better than her girlhood dreams. Drew would be with her.

Her phone's ring tone was a rude interruption. Drew stiffened, then backed away. "Go ahead and answer it," he said. "I'll wait."

"No." She dug the phone from her purse and shut it off. "From now on, people can leave a voice mail. I'll answer when it's convenient for me."

He grinned. "You really are turning over a new leaf."

"I'm trying." She moved into his arms again. "Now where were we?"

They moved to the bed and lay down facing one another, drawing out their lovemaking, exploring each other's bodies. She traced the indentation of each vertebra of his spine with her hand and ran her tongue along the curve of his ear and the strong line of his jaw. He kissed the nape of her neck and the small of her back, and teased her nipples into tight, aching buds.

Then he lay on his back and she knelt over him, guiding him into her, watching his face as he filled her, her muscles tightening around him in a surge of such pleasure she let out a cry of delight.

Hands on her hips, he guided her as she moved over him, advancing and retreating, the tension building. He moved one hand to fondle her clit, his gaze holding hers. She had never felt more vulnerable, and yet more secure.

Her climax came in waves, deep and steady, reverberating through her. His own release followed soon after, and he pulled her tightly against him as he thrust hard into her.

Afterward, they lay in each other's arms, unspeaking. Sara marveled at how each time with him was precious and yet this time she had the assurance of many more hours spent in his arms. They would make this work. She believed with all her heart that they were indeed, meant to be together.

THE *Sin on the Beach* festival finale that evening promised to be the biggest bash of the week. Bonfires blazed amidst colorful banners and tents arrayed half a mile of the beach. Live bands performed on two stages and all the popular television show's stars were on hand for autograph sessions. Sponsors handed out swag at booths up and down the sand and three bars kept everyone plied with fruity drinks and beer.

In the center of the celebration, a large stage had been erected, complete with a video screen that aired outtakes from *Sin on the Beach,* including a few from the episode filmed that week. Sara and Drew gathered with Candy and Matt and Ellie and Bill and the women squealed and hugged Ellie when she appeared in a brief scene, looking hot in a black bikini, her Queen of Evil tattoo peeking just above the waistband. They applauded when Gus made an appearance, surrounded by a bevy of bikini-clad babes.

"You looked great up there," Candy told Ellie when the screen switched to a music video.

"Filming the show was a blast," Ellie said.

"You made it more enjoyable than most shoots I've been on," Bill said, pulling her close. He and Ellie had already revealed their plans to share office space in their old neighborhood in East L.A. Ellie would manage a new, expanded Dark Gothic Roast coffee shop while Bill pursued his dream of making independent films.

As for Matt and Candy, they were a definite item. Saying she preferred to have him as a lover instead of a boss, Candy planned to devote her creativity and energy to her own marketing firm.

"And now, the moment you've all been waiting for." The video screen went black and the music faded as one of the festival organizers walked to center stage. "We're going to announce this week's grand prize winner."

The crowd cheered and applauded. Sara gripped Drew's arm. Candy crossed the fingers on both hands. "We're going to win," she said. "I know it."

Sara wasn't as confident. After reviewing their spreadsheet, she'd made the tough decision not to narc on Garth. She thought she and Candy and Ellie had enough points to beat the Santa Monica bunch—points they'd earned honestly. And there was the essay to consider. Candy had turned it in that morning and Sara and Ellie had declared it a sure winner.

Still, these things were so subjective….

"The third-place prize package of swimwear from Ocean Bay and a weekend at the Malibu Beach Inn goes to Jerry's Team from Torrance."

A happy quartet came forward to claim their prize certificates and shake hands with the announcers.

"Second place—surfboards and gear from the Surf Shack—goes to the Bayside Beach Apes."

A trio of young men, all wearing Planet of the Apes rubber masks, came forward to claim their prizes. "This is taking forever," Ellie said as the Apes posed for pictures.

"We should know after this next one," Sara said.

"First prize goes to a team that managed to earn an amazing 3,421 points," the announcer continued. "For a pair of custom Wave Runners and a margarita machine from Dave's Party House, the winner is the Santa Monica Marvels."

While everyone around them applauded and cheered, Candy leaned over to Sara. "The Marvels? They couldn't come up with a better name than that?"

"Looks like you might have won this one," Bill said.

Ellie squeezed his hand, then reached out and took hold of Candy. Sara held Candy's other hand and her breath as she waited for the final announcement.

"The Marvels had the most points," the announcer said. "But as you all know, the grand prize winner is not determined by points alone. Participants were also required to submit an essay making a case for why they should be chosen to receive the grand prize of a week's timeshare each summer in this fabulous Malibu beach house."

Images appeared of a truly swanky beach house,

with expanses of glass overlooking the ocean, a game room complete with pool table and wet bar, and an extra-large hot tub on a deck jutting out over the waves. The crowd whooped and hollered. "Can't you just see us all there?" Candy said, bouncing up and down beside Matt.

The announcer glanced at the clipboard again. "Here is a portion of the winning essay.

The Magic of Malibu lies not only in its sparkling blue waters and expanses of sandy beach, but in its status as a place apart. Here three friends came together for one week, to escape their everyday lives and have fun. But the magic of Malibu did more than help them relax. It transformed them. In one spectacular week they discovered love, expanded their horizons and set a new course for their lives. Winning the timeshare would allow them to return each year to commemorate that first life-changing week, strengthen their friendship and celebrate the place that will always be special to them all."

The announcer looked up from his clipboard. "The grand prize winner of the Malibu timeshare goes to the Java Mamas."

Sara and the others managed to keep quiet until the end, then they squealed and hugged, and rushed to the stage to claim their prize. They posed for pictures, then called the guys to join them.

As they hugged and congratulated each other, Sara interrupted them. "I've got more good news," she said.

"What is it?" Candy demanded.

Sara glanced at Drew, who grinned back at her. "I've already told Drew, but in a few months, I hope to move to Malibu permanently."

"You're not going to work for Uncle Spence anymore?" Ellie asked.

"I am, but he and I had a long talk this afternoon. We've decided to branch out. I'll take the corporate offices and relocate them here to Malibu, while he's going back to his first love, working with residential clients in L.A."

"That's perfect," Ellie said. "You can both do what you love."

"And I can be with the man I love." She looked at Drew.

Someone produced a bottle of champagne and they filled plastic flutes and toasted. "To friends," Candy said.

"To romance," Sara added.

"To *Sin on the Beach*," Ellie said. "And the perfect Malibu vacation."

* * * * *

SPECIAL EDITION®

LIFE, LOVE AND FAMILY

*These contemporary romances will strike
a chord with you as heroines juggle life
and relationships on their way to true love.*

New York Times *bestselling author*
Linda Lael Miller
*brings you a BRAND-NEW contemporary story
featuring her fan-favorite McKettrick family.*

Meg McKettrick is surprised to be reunited
with her high school flame, Brad O'Ballivan.
After enjoying a career as a country-and-
western singer, Brad aches for a home and
family...and seeing Meg again makes him
realize he still loves her. But their pride
manages to interfere with love...until an unexpected matchmaker gets involved.

*Turn the page for a sneak preview of
THE McKETTRICK WAY
by Linda Lael Miller
On sale November 20,
wherever books are sold.*

Brad shoved the truck into gear and drove to the bottom of the hill, where the road forked. Turn left, and he'd be home in five minutes. Turn right, and he was headed for Indian Rock.

He had no damn business going to Indian Rock.

He had nothing to say to Meg McKettrick, and if he never set eyes on the woman again, it would be two weeks too soon.

He turned right.

He couldn't have said why.

He just drove straight to the Dixie Dog Drive-In.

Back in the day, he and Meg used to meet at the Dixie Dog, by tacit agreement, when either of them had been away. It had been some kind of universe thing, purely intuitive.

Passing familiar landmarks, Brad told himself he ought to turn around. The old days were gone. Things had ended badly between him and Meg anyhow, and she wasn't going to be at the Dixie Dog.

He kept driving.

He rounded a bend, and there was the Dixie Dog. Its big neon sign, a giant hot dog, was all lit up and going through its corny sequence—first it was covered in red squiggles of light, meant to suggest ketchup, and then yellow, for mustard.

Brad pulled into one of the slots next to a speaker, rolled down the truck window and ordered.

A girl roller-skated out with the order about five minutes later.

When she wheeled up to the driver's window, smiling, her eyes went wide with recognition, and she dropped the tray with a clatter.

Silently Brad swore. Damn if he hadn't forgotten he was a famous country singer.

The girl, a skinny thing wearing too much eye makeup, immediately started to cry. "I'm sorry!" she sobbed, squatting to gather up the mess.

"It's okay," Brad answered quietly, leaning to look down at her, catching a glimpse of her plastic name tag. "It's okay, Mandy. No harm done."

"I'll get you another dog and a shake right away, Mr. O'Ballivan!"

"Mandy?"

She stared up at him pitifully, sniffling. Thanks to the copious tears, most of the goop on her eyes had slid south. "Yes?"

"When you go back inside, could you not mention seeing me?"

"But you're Brad O'Ballivan!"

"Yeah," he answered, suppressing a sigh. "I know."

She rolled a little closer. "You wouldn't happen to have a picture you could autograph for me, would you?"

"Not with me," Brad answered.

"You could sign this napkin, though," Mandy said. "It's only got a little chocolate on the corner."

Brad took the paper napkin and her order pen, and scrawled his name. Handed both items back through the window.

She turned and whizzed back toward the side entrance to the Dixie Dog.

Brad waited, marveling that he hadn't considered incidents like this one before he'd decided to come back home. In retrospect, it seemed shortsighted, to say the least, but the truth was, he'd expected to be— Brad O'Ballivan.

Presently Mandy skated back out again, and this time she managed to hold on to the tray.

"I didn't tell a soul!" she whispered. "But Heather and Darlene *both* asked me why my mascara was all smeared." Efficiently she hooked the tray onto the bottom edge of the window.

Brad extended payment, but Mandy shook her head.

"The boss said it's on the house, since I dumped your first order on the ground."

He smiled. "Okay, then. Thanks."

Mandy retreated, and Brad was just reaching for the food when a bright red Blazer whipped into the space beside his. The driver's door sprang open, crashing into the metal speaker, and somebody got out in a hurry.

Something quickened inside Brad.

And in the next moment Meg McKettrick was

standing practically on his running board, her blue eyes blazing.

Brad grinned. "I guess you're not over me after all," he said.

▼ *Silhouette*®

SPECIAL EDITION™

brings you a heartwarming
new McKettrick's story from

NEW YORK TIMES **BESTSELLING AUTHOR**

LINDA LAEL
MILLER

THE
McKETTRICK
Way

Meg McKettrick is surprised to be reunited
with her high school flame, Brad O'Ballivan,
who has returned home to his family's
neighboring ranch. After seeing Meg again,
Brad realizes he still loves her. But the pride
of both manage to interfere with love...until
an unexpected matchmaker gets involved.

—— McKettrick Women ——

Available December wherever you buy books.

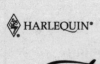

Mediterranean
N I G H T S™

*Experience glamour, elegance, mystery
and romance aboard the high seas....*

Coming in December 2007...

A PERFECT MARRIAGE?

by
Cindi Myers

Is there such a thing as a perfect marriage?

Trying to recapture the magic of their marriage,
Katherine Stamos and her husband, Charles, take
a cruise aboard *Alexandra's Dream*. Once aboard
ship, it's still hard to leave their work behind and
much of what Katherine needs to hear remains
unsaid. Is it too late to find the excitement of love
after twenty years of marriage?

www.eHarlequin.com

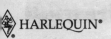

HARLEQUIN®

American ★ Romance®

Kate Merrill had grown up convinced
that the most attractive men were incapable
of ever settling down. Yet the harder she
resisted the superstar photographer
Tyler Nichols, the more persistent the
handsome world traveler became.
So by the time Christmas arrived, there
was only one wish on her holiday list—
that she was wrong!

LOOK FOR

THE CHRISTMAS DATE

BY

Michele Dunaway

Available December
wherever you buy books

REQUEST YOUR FREE BOOKS

2 FREE NOVELS PLUS 2 FREE GIFTS!

HARLEQUIN®

Blaze

Red-hot reads.

YES! Please send me 2 FREE Harlequin® Blaze® novels and my 2 FREE gifts. After receiving them, if I don't wish to receive any more books, I can return the shipping statement marked "cancel." If I don't cancel, I will receive 6 brand-new novels every month and be billed just $3.99 per book in the U.S., or $4.47 per book in Canada, plus 25¢ shipping and handling per book and applicable taxes, if any*. That's a savings of at least 15% off the cover price! I understand that accepting the 2 free books and gifts places me under no obligation to buy anything. I can always return a shipment and cancel at any time. Even if I never buy another book from Harlequin, the two free books and gifts are mine to keep forever.

151 HDN EF3W   351 HDN EF3X

Name	(PLEASE PRINT)	
Address		Apt.
City	State/Prov.	Zip/Postal Code

Signature (if under 18, a parent or guardian must sign)

Mail to the Harlequin Reader Service®:
IN U.S.A.: P.O. Box 1867, Buffalo, NY 14240-1867
IN CANADA: P.O. Box 609, Fort Erie, Ontario L2A 5X3

Not valid to current Harlequin Blaze subscribers.

Want to try two free books from another line?
Call 1-800-873-8635 or visit www.morefreebooks.com.

* Terms and prices subject to change without notice. NY residents add applicable sales tax. Canadian residents will be charged applicable provincial taxes and GST. This offer is limited to one order per household. All orders subject to approval. Credit or debit balances in a customer's account(s) may be offset by any other outstanding balance owed by or to the customer. Please allow 4 to 6 weeks for delivery.

Your Privacy: Harlequin is committed to protecting your privacy. Our Privacy Policy is available online at www.eHarlequin.com or upon request from the Reader Service. From time to time we make our lists of customers available to reputable firms who may have a product or service of interest to you. If you would prefer we not share your name and address, please check here. ☐

HB

Get ready to meet

THREE WISE WOMEN

with stories by

DONNA BIRDSELL,
LISA CHILDS

and

SUSAN CROSBY.

Don't miss these three unforgettable stories
about modern-day women and the love
and new lives they find on Christmas.

Look for *Three Wise Women*
Available December wherever you buy books.

Blaze™

COMING NEXT MONTH

#363 A BLAZING LITTLE CHRISTMAS Jacquie D'Alessandro, Joanne Rock, Kathleen O'Reilly
A sizzling Christmas anthology
When a freak snowstorm strands three couples at the Timberline Lodge for the holidays, anything is possible...including incredible sex! Cozy up to these sizzling Christmas stories that prove that a "blazing ever after" is the best gift of all....

#364 STROKES OF MIDNIGHT Hope Tarr
The Wrong Bed
When author Becky Stone's horoscope predicted that the New Year would bring her great things, she never expected the first thing she'd experience would be *a great one-night stand!* Or that her New Year's fling would last the whole year through....

#365 TALKING IN YOUR SLEEP... Samantha Hunter
It's almost Christmas and all Rafe Moore can hear...is sexy whispering right in his ear. Next-door neighbor Joy Clarke is talking in her sleep and it's keeping Rafe up at night. Rafe's ready to explore her whispered desires. Problem is, in the light of day, Joy doesn't recall a thing!

#366 BABY, IT'S COLD OUTSIDE Cathy Yardley
And that's why Colin Reeves and Emily Stanfield head indoors—then it's sparks, sensual heat and hot times ahead! But will their private holiday hometown reunion last longer than forty-eight delicious hours in bed?

#367 THE BIG HEAT Jennifer LaBrecque
Big, Bad Bounty Hunters, Bk. 2
When Cade Stone agreed to keep an eye on smart-mouthed Sunny Templeton, he figured it wouldn't be too hard. After all, all she'd done was try to take out a politician. Who wouldn't do the same thing? Cade knew she wasn't a threat to jump bail. Too bad he hadn't counted on her wanting to jump him....

#368 WHAT SHE *REALLY* WANTS FOR CHRISTMAS Debbi Rawlins
Million Dollar Secrets, Bk. 6
Liza Skinner, lottery winner wannabe, *thinks* she knows the kind of guy she should be with, but is she ever wrong! Dr. Evan Gann is just the one to show her that a buttoned-down type can have a wild side and still come through for her when she needs him most....

www.eHarlequin.com

HBCNM11